# The Mission
## Collection

**Tara Basi**

# The Mission

# Chapter One – Escape

I'm the sausage in the roll, the mole in the hole, the pod in the bay.

On I wriggle.

Stopping occasionally to nibble my NOC-supplied sandwich. It's my favourite: miso paste and cherry jam on sourdough.

After the chaos of the ward, I'm enjoying the snug fit, the steady thrum and the dark of the hospital's air vents.

If it weren't for the Mission, I'd stay here.

The sandwich is finished. Goodbye, sandwich.

Up ahead, a grille marks the first waypoint: the bin room.

I listen carefully: sweet silence.

Down I drop and lightly land and slip past the bins to listen at the door.

More soundless goodness.

The door is cracked; the corridor is dark.

The deranged NOC's escape plan is working, so far.

A little way ahead is the door to the stairs.

With my back against the wall, I crouch and slide like a ninja crab.

Out of the dark, a bobbing light approaches.

I freeze.

"You lost, Kevin?" the bobbing light asks.

I shake my head. "Exercising."

"It's three a.m., Kevin."

"Doctor Bird said it's never too late to start exercising."

"The TV doctor? She's hot. Okay, Kevin. See you later."

The bobbing light departs.

Normal breathing is resumed.

Onwards, on wobbly hands and knees.

The door to the stairwell is unlocked, just as NOC promised.

Backwards, step by step, I descend till there are no more steps. I've arrived at the door to the basement carpark.

The lower levels are patrolled by the security elite.

Namely, Bob: an athletic, ex-military man with an eyepatch and a plastic hearing aid, only a little smaller than his head. He is armed with a cattle prod.

Everyone is scared of Bob. Few have ever seen him.

I must be extra stealthy.

Slippers are slipped and stowed in my dressing gown pockets.

Slowly, carefully, the basement carpark door is teased open.

It creaks and squeals in alarm.

Bob will surely be alerted and must be racing towards me with his crackling baton.

I don't know what to do. Should I flee back to the ward?

Before I can decide, the half-open door is wrenched from my grasp.

"Where you been, Kevin? I've been shitting myself."

It's NOC. My hands fly to my ears.

"Did I frighten you, sweetie dumpling? Mandy's so vewy sowy. Are you okay, baby?"

The noise coming out of her mouth is so loud. Bob must surely hear her?

I put a finger to my lips.

NOC is staring at me.

I think she looks hungry.

NOC grabs me in a terrible embrace and squeezes hard.

"Bob?" I whisper, hoping she'll stop crushing me and focus on our escape.

"God, you're gorgeous."

"Bob?" I hiss, wondering if she even understands the danger we're in.

"Who, babe?"

"Bob! Bob! Bob!"

Thankfully, she releases me. "Oh, Bob. Got the chop. The cuts, babe."

NOC has killed Bob. She is deranged and homicidal.

"Kevin, we gotta get going. Slippers on, babe. footrest's a bit greasy. Here."

NOC hands me a motorcycle helmet.

My head is inside in a flash. It dampens the effects of her screeching.

NOC revs her scooter.

Carefully, I mount, and without any warning, she speeds off.

I'm forced to grab hold of her squishy parts. It's disgusting.

The NOC squeezes my hand, pressing my palm even more tightly against her body.

We both moan, somehow differently, and the scooter carries us away.

I am free and it's very scary. Such responsibility, and we've already lost a potential Convert. Poor Bob.

Disregarding our speed of travel and the road ahead, NOC twists her neck and lifts her visor to look at me. "Your old place first? Right, babe?"

I nod furiously and push her face back in the direction of travel.

NOC whimpers and tries to lick my fingers.

I snatch them away before she can bite anything off. She's looking hungrier.

We burrow through the night at great speed, my white pyjamas billowing like clouds against the fluttering blue of my dressing gown.

A disgusting image. I hate bright colours.

"We're here, Kevin."

Indeed, we are.

I gladly untangle myself from NOC, dismount and head to the house. The key is under the mat. Inside, everything is as I remember. Dark and ripe.

Memories of the Kevin litter the room.

From the time before my arrival and after the possession.

The Kevin has been an acceptable host.

The NOC barely deserves the title.

The all-important laptop, phone, big black over-ear cans and shades are where I left them. I don black jeans, black tee-shirt, black hoodie and black trainers.

I re-join NOC, who's helmetless and fiddling with her phone.

"Kevin–"

Two fingers pressed to my helmet visor silence her. I stare fixedly at her phone.

NOC follows the direction of my gaze and then looks at me. Her eyebrows dance about her face, no doubt conveying some meaning.

I usually guess wrong, unless her eyes are leaking and she wails.

I nod vigorously in the direction of her mobile and hold out my hand.

Her eyes widen and her lips wriggle, like cavorting worms, before she turns it over.

I pair it with my own, download the Mission app and return it. With a swipe and a tap, I open up the Communication window on my own handset.

Number One Convert, this is a test message. Please confirm receipt. The Missionary.

NOC is startled by the deep rumble her phone makes. "What the fuck you done to my phone, Kevin? Why's it making that horrible noise? I ain't got no insurance, Kev."

In silence, I fold my arms.

NOC lets out a lot of air then stabs at her phone with a bright red nail. Her head bends low, and the phone is brought very close to her face. "You doing this, honey-bun? Who's the Missionary? What's a Number One Convert? Is that me, babe? That why you calling me NOC? Am I your number one? That's so cute. Is this like a new game?"

Even through my helmet, her voice is awfully grating. I dip my head towards her phone.

More air is discharged; her eyebrows battle each other. Rapid, two-finger nail-tapping begins. It goes on for some time.

God, you're really hot when you're all ordering me about and shit. But, babes, we gotta get out of here!!!!!!! XXXXXX Mandy! Your Number One!

Even her text message is loud. Though she's right; we should depart while it's still dark, and I'm anxious to meet the First Tier Converts that NOC has identified. They'll be the great inspirational thought leaders who will take the Mission to the masses.

We remount her scooter.

The NOC pulls my arms tightly around her waist and off we shoot. "Baby, don't be shy; squeeze harder. That's it, baby. Oh, baby."

I shudder.
She giggles.

## Chapter Two – Love is ... Smelly

It was love at first sniff. Kevin filled up my nose with sweetness and hotness and cherry blossom. It was a normal shitty day at the Prince Albert Memorial Psychiatric Hospital. Stepped through those stupid doors that never open fast enough, and his smell hit me. Wow. It was like nothing I'd never sniffed before. Best way I can describe it is, you know when you watch those sexy perfume ads, with all those hot people getting off on something, like Gold Jasmine Sweat? It was like that. Not like Gold Jasmine Sweat actually smells, cos that stuff all smells the same, and it's usually shit. Especially if it's, like, super discounted in January, cos the celeb on the bottle's gone and topped themselves or been caught kiddie fiddling. Though, to be fair, January's when I usually stock up. Can't afford full price. No, it's not that smell. It's the smell you imagine when you're watching the vid. When they're getting all sexy and dropping slippery dresses and silky shirts. That smell. The smell you never get out of the bottle.

They'd wheeled Kevin into the hospital just a couple of minutes before I'd arrived for my shift. Well, first thing I ask is ... what's that gorgeous smell?

"Hi, Mandy, some new loony. You like that stink? Eww!"

They found Kevin sitting in his lounge playing a videogame. He'd been playing straight for a month. Only stopped to pop into the hall toilet. And, even then, he kept the door open, so he could keep an eye on the screen. They say he never slept. He used his mum's card to get food and stuff delivered.

The Tesco guy brought it right into the lounge for him. That's how they know a bit about what Kevin got up to after his mum died. It was usually the same Tesco guy. Came at all hours. They never spoke. Tesco guy just stacked up the stuff around Kevin's chair. If the Tesco guy wasn't busy, he sat in the back for a while and watched Kevin play. Tesco guy said Kevin was a gaming genius. Especially since he was playing some game he'd written himself. Tesco guy said it was a really weird game, all about some galactic mission to convert the heathens. Or some such super brainy shit.

Anyhow, all Kevin ever ordered was bottled water and little metal packets of miso soup. No idea what that was when they told me. Found out later; gave it a try. Horrible shit. Essential ingredient, though. Bit pongy on its own. And the Tesco guy brought cherries. Fresh, mind. So Kevin had this electric kettle by his chair and water and stacks of plastic cups. When he got hungry, he'd be eating cherries out of a big crate or making soup.

When they broke in, the lounge floor was knee deep in cherry pips, cherry stalks, torn silvery miso packets, plastic cups, plastic water bottles. And the smell. Well, you know what I think about that gorgeous perfume. Can't say everybody liked it. Kevin didn't say anything when they came for him. Even when they strapped him to a trolley and wheeled him out. Couldn't get the game's thingummy-jig out of his hands.

First time I saw Kevin – bang! Right between the legs! Oh. My. God. That boy was Love Island fit.

His mum was in the freezer.

Nothing untoward, like. All natural. Kevin was just tidying up.

Bloody doctors decided he was a bit loopy and difficult and weird and stuffed him full of nasty drugs. Killed my future boyfriend chances that did. Wasn't standing for that. I'm a bit of a medical expert. Been a receptionist at the hospital for six months and I've picked up a lot. And I got the computer. You come in with a bit of depression and give me any lip, you'll be going home chemically castrated.

And I talked to my friend Liz. She's so clever. Top Morrisons' checkout girl three years running. Liz, she told me 'bout this site – Unbelievable Medical Cures Right Now Without Medicine or Doctors. It's fantastic, it's got all this great advice, and it's basically saying doctors are just experimenting on us. They ain't got a fucking clue. And Big Pharma just wants to sell as much shit as they can, and they got no idea what it's doing to our insides.

I've seen what goes on in that hospital. Everyone gets worse and, with the cuts, they gets worse quicker. So, I have a meeting with Liz and the other top medical guy I know: the hospital DJ, Freddy. I explains my diagnoses – seriously, how can anyone that hot be crazy? – and immediately we decided, like almost unanimously (Liz abstains), we're going to save Kevin.

Obviously, now I know it was a fucking stupid, dangerously bad idea.

## Chapter Three – Iconic

My hideout's very nice.

One room, dark and woody.

There's a cot and a kettle and a bench and a potty.

I've been here many days.

NOC is overdue.

A few nights ago, we mounted NOC's scooter to go meet the candidates.

Scary.

Necessary.

NOC's First Tier Convert candidates are good people.

They listened attentively to my Rapture or Reset sermon.

Fierce Liz will make an indomitable Convertor.

Gentle, devoted Freddy is truly enraptured.

I've been very busy.

The Reset part of the Mission app is complete. I pray it will never have to be used.

Many icons have been signed for Freddy.

Freddy says many want to donate.

Freddy suggested auto-pay-donations for the Mission app.

I suggested 1p.

Freddy bobbled his head and smiled.

Freddy will deal with the details.

He's a selfless First Tier Convert.

Now I wait.

Turn, step, pace, twirl.

Where is NOC?

Step, spin, hop, dip, skipity, skip, skip.

She's late.

Tickity, tockty, tick, tick.

Has NOC not understood the urgency?

Bang! Bang!

"Babes, you decent? Don't mind if you ain't!"

The NOC's giggles rattle my teeth.

Cans and shades are donned. "NOC may enter."

"Jesus, babe, why you always in the dark? Open the curtains, babe."

"Late. Go."

"We got time, babe. Market don't start till eight a.m. Freddy needs time to set up."

NOC flings open the sack curtains on my two little windows.

Sometimes I hate NOC. "Seen. Taken back!"

"What, babe?"

NOC stares.

I wait.

There is often a lag between my speaking and NOC understanding, as though we are communicating over millions of miles.

If only it were true.

"Oh, the hospital? No probs, babes. You's officially ... discharged into the community. I'm like receptionist god. That computer's my bitch, babe."

NOC has hacking skills? Unfathomable creature.

"You like my dad's shed, babes? Mum never comes in here. Not after ..." NOC nods towards the ceiling.

I spy a hook.

NOC cricks her head to one side, sticks out her tongue and gurgles like a drain.

NOC strangled and gutted her own father?

NOC sighs. "Mum and Dad used to be, like, huge Essex porn stars. Before proper phones and shit. Didn't know till I asked my mum for some advanced sex-ed, like threesome spooning etiquette or some such bollocks. Anyway, she gives me one of their old VHS tapes. Colchester Cocksuckers Banging in Basildon. Now that was educational. A bit weird, though, getting turned on by your mum and dad with other people. Proper fit they were back then. Dad was seriously hung and Mum had fantastic knockers. Not now, like. You know, if my knockers ever got like Mum's, I'd have them Jolied – Angelina, like. So anyways, Dad couldn't get it up anymore. Wore it out, I guess. Comes down here and offs himself. I was like knee-high to a toilet brush back then. Hardly knew the guy. Sad though. There was this one film they did with a horse–"

My ears can't take anymore.

I cover NOC's mouth with my own.

Why? Why am I doing this?

A trace of the Kevin? A ghost in the host?

It's too late to escape.

NOC has me in a crushing grip.

I feel like toothpaste.

Who knows what she'll squeeze out.

More horror.

NOC is cleaning my teeth with her tongue.

Her body undulates like a goat swallowing python.

I can't breathe.

"Oh, babe, I think I came. God, that was so fucking hot."

I'm saved.

NOC has collapsed against the bench; her front parts have become stormy sea buoys.

"Go! Late! Mission!"

"Yeah, babes, okay … but you ain't getting any sleep tonight."

NOC looks ravenous.

What have I done?

We ride atop NOC's scooter. Our two hearts thump like a hammer banging a nail.

Am I the nail? Is NOC the hammer?

We fly by many icons, on walls, in shop windows.

Busy Freddy.

At the market, everything is tossed about like dirty laundry, and I'm the odd sock.

The helmet can't come off, my brain will evaporate.

Too many humans, too much noise, and the stained-glass sky is raining splinters.

I crawl under the stall. It's a little better.

NOC is shouting at me.

"Kevin, pumpkin, helmet off; people want to see you."

My head wibble-wobbles in protest.

"Mission, babes. For the Mission."

NOC is right.

Without Rapture, there is only Reset.

Helmet off, cans and glasses on, hoodie up.

NOC drags me to my feet to stand behind the stall.

There's a lot of screaming.

I see six shoes.

NOC's to the left.

Freddy's pink sneakers to the right.

The stall is overflowing with icons.

NOC gently lifts my chin.

Eyes tight shut.

The screams get louder.

Freddy sermonises.

"Right, girls, it's fifteen quid for the app. Ten quid for a signed poster. Stop pushing, bitches. Hey, slag, you touch that poster, you bought that poster."

"Drop dead, faggot."

Unusual sermon.

Eyes nailed shut.

Screams upon screams.

Two fat slugs have slid into my jean pockets and are wriggling everywhere.

I'm stupefied with fear.

It's NOC and Freddy.

They're looking for my phone.

In all the wrong places.

Very wrong places.

Slap, slap handies away.

I remove the phone.

"Awe! I was having fun, Kev. The slags could've waited. Okay … hold it out. That's it, babe."

Freddy is eulogising.

"Fifteen quid, and it's phone-touching only, love, or Mandy here's gonna rip a tit off and then I'm gonna make you eat it."

"Fuck off, mister."

There's a nudge on my phone, and I hear the low rumble of a successful download.

"How much for a snog?"

"No one's fucking snogging my boyfriend except me. On your bike, you little whore."

"Fuck off yourself."

Thwack! Howl!

"Next!" Freddy yells.

This is not how Conversions usually work.

I can't help feeling … satisfied.

Maybe a little peek.

Definitely a big shriek.

Hundreds of human females lined up.

Eyes get shut till I'm back on NOC's scooter heading home.

Though I shouldn't like to do it again, there were hundreds of Conversions today.

A toasty smile warms my face and gently spreads.

"Can't wait to get you home, babe. I'm, like, churning down there."

My smile freezes over.

## Chapter Four – Brain Dicked

Saved Kevin isn't quite like I'd imagined. Pro. He's even sexier. There's this, like, pumped intensity about him. And he's all mysterious and brainy. It's so romantic and super horny. Then there's the cons. He doesn't like talking to me, looking at me, touching me, which is bang out of order frustrating. Like I'm Miley with that bloody big, sexy wrecking ball, but it won't let me on. See, I ain't never known any hot bloke who could keep his hands off me for more than ten seconds. Which is normal. Not like I'm boasting or nothing, but I'm a nine-and-a-half, easy. Everyone says so. Really. I could be a model. Glamour, like. My tits are too big for the other kind. That's what they said down the agency. Didn't fancy it. Mum's like, bloody stupid cow, what else you gonna do? Not nice.

Even Liz does it. We'll be having a serious conversation about Kardashian's latest bum pic and her eyes have drifted down to my nipples. "Liz!" I say. And she's like, "Mandy, I'm all sorry and everything," and she's just thinking of getting hers done. Which is believable. Hers look like a couple of peanuts in a sock. Sometimes, Liz gets this really weird, dopey, slippery look when she's eyeballing my boobs. Don't think she even realises it.

I don't want to get my boobs out for money. Then it's like, I'm my boobs. They're in the room first, they get noticed first, and whatever's going on a bit higher up and following right behind is boring. Hot guys saying, 'Damn them some super-fine bitch bags on Mandy' ain't enough. What I wanted was an AND. A big AND. Like Kim's ANDs.

That's gorgeous Mandy with her own line in thongs AND monogrammed rubbers, AND she's got some super-fine bitch bags.

Kevin saw that; he wasn't staring at them all the time, or at any time. God, I'm so itchy down there every time I think about him. Maybe I should have made the first move, something subtle, like. Maybe stuck my tongue in his ear, playfully. You know? I thought I'd ask Liz. Freddy too; he knows his guys.

He's had enough of them. Given how things went, I never did.

That's got me thinking about the first time they met Kevin.

"Freddy, Liz, you got to give me your phones."

"What the hell, Mandy girl? Why you want our phones? Where's this Kevin anyway? You busted him out or what? The feds chasing him? They got a satellite on your ass?"

Freddy's always questioning things. Is the earth really flat? Crazy shit like that.

"Gee, Mandy, I gotta lot of private stuff on my phone. You know?"

"Yeah, like hundreds of snatch pics. Why you got no proper dicks on your phone, Liz? What's wrong with you, girl? Hand 'em over now or Kevin ain't coming in. You'll get 'em back."

There was a bit more banter before they gave them up. Liz and Freddy were pumped about meeting Kevin. You know, after everything I'd been telling them. We got together in this little storeroom above a tiny Tesco Metro that basically only sold booze, fags, KY and rubbers. Liz sometimes did overnighters in the place. Pay's good. Customers were a bit dodgy, but Liz can take care of herself. She's muscly. Does weights, boxing. Shoots up with testy. Ain't doing nothing for her tits, though. Only making them look smaller, if you ask me. Straight up, Liz's a five, at best. The Mohican, the face piercings and the neck tatts didn't help.

Popped outside, Kevin did his magic with the phones and sends me back in.

"Here, you got a text."

"Mandy, why's it doing that? It's like a bloody rabbit turned up to ten."

"Never mind, Liz. That's just, like, a side bonus."

"Where's this text, girl? Ain't no text."

"Freddy, you dick, it's that blue icon flashing thingy. Hit it."

"Mandy, you poxed my phone?"

"Freddy, only thing poxed around here is your dick."

"What's it do, this Mission app? Kevin done this?"

"Yeah, Liz. It's his. He wrote it. It's safe. Look. See, got it on my phone. Now will you twats just bang on?"

Potential First Tier Convert Candidates. The Rapture is coming. The Missionary.

"Kevin doing this? He's a fucking loony. You said he was better."

"Jesus, Mandy, what's this crap? You want me to sort the fucker out?"

"Freddy, Liz. Stop going all Britney on me and listen. Kevin's got plans. Big plans."

After that, Kevin came in, looking shit hot. You know? All in black, hoodie up, over massive cans, and these super-slick, wraparound shades. He starts explaining. For me, it gets real boring real fast and anyways I'm a bit distracted. His mouth's so fucking sexy. All I could think about was sitting on his face.

At the time, I thought it went okay, and everyone seemed really keen on the Mission.

Should have seen the signs. Whole time Kev's talking, Liz's like cracking walnuts with her eyelids and chewing mouldy lemons. And Freddy's lips couldn't have got any more licked, like he's listening to a Calvin Klein boxer's model without the boxers. But Freddy got really interested in the Mission game.

It was a bloody stupid game, if you ask me. Course, wouldn't say that now. Back then I thought it was a load of bollocks about collecting merit thingies, so you can get to mothership space heaven Rapture, and jumping over Reset demons and Reset hellfire and shit. I said to Freddy, later and whispery, like, so Kevin didn't hear, "No one's gonna want to play that crap."

I was, like, brain dicked back then. Didn't see it coming. Not at all.

At least now I got lots of ANDs.

Mandy's Queen of Essex; AND next week her army's invading Fucked, aka Suffolk; AND she's got gorgeous tits.

I suppose that's something. Innit?

## Chapter Five – Shard

My one-room, dark and woody hideout has been moved.

The Shed is at the top of the Shard now.

Otherwise, nothing has changed.

There's still a cot and a kettle and a bench and a potty.

I need height for the Signal.

The First Tier Converts have been very productive.

Conversion rates are accelerating.

Freddy is a gentle and devoted disciple.

Liz is fiercely determined, more so recently.

NOC only appears interested in Mondays and getting ready for Mondays.

For the wellbeing of the Kevin host, I tolerate Mondays.

Today is our anniversary.

Thankfully, it's not a Monday.

More than a year has passed since I took possession of the Kevin.

And exactly one year since NOC freed me.

We are celebrating, and there is much to celebrate.

Freddy and I are standing by the Shed, which is by the pool.

At night, I sometimes lie in the pool and stare at the stars through the great windows.

Looking for home.

In the daytime, I keep to the Shed.

It's night.

Liz and NOC are in the pool.

They are squealing and laughing and splashing.

Odd, to hear Liz laughing.

I hope she is well.

Freddy is always sniffing and rubbing his nose.

I hope he is well.

He flagellates himself so, being overburdened with much shiny metal.

"The Pope wants an audience."

Freddy occasionally brings potential Converts to visit the Shed.

They kneel outside.

I whisper my sermon through the Shed's keyhole.

So, its tolerable, occasionally.

"You shitting us, Freddy? The Pope? Seriously?"

NOC is always doubting.

It's not becoming of an NOC.

Perhaps I should withhold a Monday, as punishment.

The Kevin may suffer ill-effects.

I must not risk the Kevin.

"That stuck-up bitch Swifty was on her knees at that fucking keyhole last week. She's got more followers than the Pope. Ain't that right, Freddy?"

Liz is so positive.

"Hey, Kev, how we doing? Mission-wise? Nearly done?"

Of late, Liz is always asking that question.

"Twenty-five percent."

Liz hoots and cheers.

NOC shrieks, climbs out of the pool and runs inside.

"So, Kev, Pope next week? Monday?"

Why is NOC so upset? The Mission is going so well.

Or is it? Perhaps NOC thinks we could be doing better. She may be right.

I do not want to upset her further. "Not Monday, Freddy."

# Chapter Six – Pussy Whipped

After that first trip to Freddy's stall, Kevin refused to leave the Shed for a week. It was obvious he wouldn't be doing any more personal appearances. So, Freddy started dressing up faggot boys like Kevin. The clone Kevins were doing Conversions all over Essex. Obviously, it wasn't the only reason he was dressing them up like Kevin. Didn't bother me as long as he kept his hands off the real thing.

And in the massive Morrisons outside Billericay, all the checkouts were doing Conversions. God knows how Liz managed that, and God knows why. I mean it was pretty obvious by then that she didn't even like Kevin and cared fuck all about the Mission. I thought it was the dosh. There was so much, I could've had my boobs done every bloody week.

Nowadays, some people says it was all my fault, what happened. Course, thems people is soon regretting opening their fat gobs. Nothing personal, just the times we live in. Like Liz says, its treasonous and I'm queen, so they gotta be punished. Me, you know, I'd give 'em a good bollocking and lock 'em up for a bit. Liz, she's a bit more hardcore, so they mostly being beheaded. The lucky ones.

People think I had it cushy back then. They got no clue. When I was around Kevin, it was like there was an orgy going on in my thong and I wasn't invited. It never got any better, even when he let me do it. I've had really fit guys pounding away for hours and all I got was friction burns. When Kevin kissed me, my pussy went off like a nuclear bomb. It was crazy. And it never eased off; it just got better and better and better. I was totally addicted to the Missionary. Can't say I paid much attention to the Mission.

Didn't help that after that first massive, boom-bang kiss, he'd only do it with me once a week, on Mondays. He was very strict about that. Drove me nuts. Like Kim being limited to one husband. I mean, how crazy would that be? In-between, nothing. Nada, fuck all. Kev didn't allow no touching, no little kisses. Jesus, I tried to hold his hand once, mid-week, and he had, like, a spazzy fit.

So that's probably why it happened.

Me and Liz were having a proper girly night out. I was necking the vintage prosecco; she was downing pints of Guinness. Having great fun telling hot guys trying it on to fuck off and wetting our pants every time we got onto the subject of the Mission. Liz had less clue than me what the fuck Kevin was going on about.

"Mandy, you think Freddy's got any idea what Kev's Mission is?"

"Liz, you taking the piss? Only things Freddy understands is cock, bum, coke and dosh."

The Guinness and prosecco gets sprayed everywhere.

"Want to hear something really crazy, Mandy?"

"What?"

"Most of the dumb fuck Converts think it's real."

"Real? What you mean, Liz?"

"Like the whole thing, the Reset hellfire, the Rapture mothership. Like it's really gonna happen."

I was a bit gobsmacked for a second. "Come on, Liz, no one's that dumb. Next you'll be telling me they believe Kevin really is an alien from outer space and stuff."

Liz nodded.

Then we both, like, exploded with giggles and drank a whole lot more.

Out of the blue, Liz grabs a boob and kisses me. Not like no pecky pecky thing. Oh no, this was snakey and deep.

Now, I don't mind a bit of pussy, now and again. Makes a nice change. Personally, I'm partial to a Chinese. Like Linda Sin, down the salon. I mean she's fucking smoking, a nine at least, and that girl had a golden tongue. What Liz obviously didn't understand is that it ain't natural for a nine and a half like myself to be messing with anything less than a nine, pussy or cock. And there's no getting away from it. Liz is barely a five. It just goes against nature. And besides, I wanted to be good for Kevin. Hadn't looked at no one else, hadn't been with no one else since we'd hooked up.

But.

The next Kevin fuck was six days away, and the last one had been so good I'd cried. I mean literally, the tears were just pouring out of my head. I knew then, I didn't just lust after

Kevin. I loved the boy. Really loved him. But there's the itch. The seven-day itch, and God it needed scratching.

So, it was frustration and the prosecco and all sorts of confusing shit that made me forget that Liz was only a five and that I loved Kevin. And maybe I kind of thought it'd be alright, just the once, cos we're both on the Mission.

Liz was bloody good. Five or not. I think, in a weird way, it was all that metal shit in her lips and tongue. But mainly it was because Kevin don't do down, and I imagined it was him doing me. Probably would have all been fine if I hadn't, like, grabbed her Mohican at the end and yelled out Kevin's name.

Liz went fucking ballistic. It took a long time to lick her down. Then, I sort of promised that once the Mission was done we'd be a proper threesome, and in-between I'd let her, like, do me now and again.

That's all sorted, I thought. An occasional with Liz wouldn't feel like cheating, more of a pity fuck really. And sometimes my pussy wasn't taking no for an answer and you get bored with plastic.

But no way was I sharing Kevin with Liz. Maybe a Linda Sin type, if Kevin was up for it. Definitely not a five, piercings or no piercings. And I reckoned it was never going to happen anyway. Kevin told me once that the Mission would only be complete when he'd Converted half the population. It sounded crazy to me when I thought he was only talking about Essex. Oh no, Kevin said, the whole world. In your dreams, Liz. Proper sorted.

More like royally unsorted.

## Chapter Seven – Reset

In thirty seconds, I must leave the Kevin.

The sights and sounds are dreadful.

It is hard to focus on sending a last message to NOC.

I shall miss NOC.

I have grown very fond of her, despite her murderous inclinations and bouts of insanity.

I shall even miss Mondays.

I shall miss Freddy and Liz.

I do not blame Liz.

She was only celebrating.

Accidents happen.

Are there faces flashing by?

Staring at me?

Perhaps it's my own face, reflected over and over?

In seconds, there will be no host.

Without a host, there can be no Missionary.

Without a Missionary, there can be no Mission.

It happens.

The life of a Missionary is perilous.

Most fail and fail often.

After my last message to NOC, I shall Reset this world.

That is the reckoning.

A new Missionary in a new millennium will try again.

And the reckoning will be remembered; the task made a little easier.

Some worlds are Reset many times before they understand.

It's sad but necessary.

Poor Kevin.

He cannot be saved.

There, the final message to NOC is sent.

My outlook is spinning ever faster, blurring into abstract shapes and bleeding colours.

Not unpretty.

A whirlwind has swallowed my head.

The Shed is following me down, only a little way behind.

The poor thing is coming apart.

The potty and the kettle fly out of the little windows.

The door comes off.

Is that Freddy tumbling out?

I wave at Freddy.

He waves back, with all of his limbs.

Poor Freddy. Goodbye Freddy.

Only a few seconds left.

The Reset is released.

The Signal is sent.

God will recall the mothership of Rapture.

Time to go home and await the next Mission.

Sometimes I succeed.

Sometimes.

## Chapter Eight – What the Fuck Day?

Course people don't blame Kevin. Some blames me. It was me what pussy blocked their road to heaven. Those dicks are mainly in Suffolk. Next week they's getting royally shafted. Nobody blames Liz. Which is properly fucked up. How can they not blame Liz? I was, like, an innocent bystander. If my dog bit a kid's head off, whose bleedin' fault is it? It's the fucking dog's. Obviously. See any bits of kiddy brain stuck between my teeth? No, you don't.

Did I see it coming? Well, kinda. Soon as Kevin announced the Mission was 99.9% done and tomorrow we'd be totally done, things went to shit. First Freddy is, like, "No way, man! We's still expanding in Russia and China and we can't stop now," and how he's nearly saved up enough to buy Columbia. And Liz is right up in my face. Wants to tell Kev about us and come to Mondays, and tomorrow's Monday. Going on and on about how I promised. She was really getting on my tits. Maybe I could have, you know, let her down easier, instead of telling her to fuck off and die, and she's only a five, and she's never getting between me and Kevs in any kind of way.

So next day, when we're all supposed to be celebrating, Freddy's in a total sulk and coked up to the max. Liz turns up late with a big bag and a nasty look. I'm kinda feeling okay. It was good to finally tell Liz what I really thought. Besides, the pity fucks weren't doing it for me anymore. And it was a Monday!

Kevin is smiling like a bloody lighthouse. He's talking some shit about calling in the mothership and starting up the Rapture.

That's when Liz pulls out this massive fucking machine gun and starts spraying bullets and screaming that if she can't do me then no one's doing me. Which, for a couple of seconds, was really flattering. Made me feel like a proper ten, to have someone go batshit crazy over you.

Freddy's screaming that he doesn't want to do me, which is obvious. Duh!

Bullets are whizzing everywhere, and Kevin's standing there like a moron and smiling like a moron.

Freddy flings himself inside the Shed. I flings myself towards Kevin, you know, to save the idiot, but I slips and falls into the pool. Next thing, there's, like, a hurricane, my ears pop big time, and then the hurricane and the shooting stopped. I took a peek. Liz was sitting on the diving board crying her eyes out. One of the huge windows is smashed. Kevin's gone. The Shed's gone. Freddy's gone.

What the fuck?

It took us ages to get down those bastard Shard stairs in the bloody dark. Blubbering all the way, "Where's Kevin? Where's my baby gone?" I was a complete mess. Imagine if both Kim's tits had exploded and killed her latest husband. Yeah, it was that bad. Couldn't have survived those first couple of weeks without Liz.

The What the Fuck Day was fucking awful.

People think it sort of came a lot later. It didn't. By my reckoning, it happened as soon as my lovely Kevin got splattered like a paintball. Why else were the sodding Shard lifts not working? When we got to the bottom, there was nothing left, just a little, bloody crater and a few bits of Shed. People paid a fortune for a bit of that Shed. Some idiot gave Liz four cows and a bag of silver for a bit of wood she'd hacked off an old toilet seat.

After a couple of months, me and Liz made up. I needed someone with big arms and a machine gun, and she was still crazy about me and genuinely sorry about Kevin and Freddy.

Everyone started calling me the Madonna. Didn't like that. Who wants to be named after some grandma who sings like a drunk slut at bad karaoke and dances like a bloody arthritic with knackered hips?

"Call me Queen," I said.

"Queen of Hearts?" they asked.

"No, you chumps. Queen of Essex, TOWIE style."

Some prick started whining on about how London ain't even in Essex.

"It is now," I says.

Liz sorted them out. She's bloody good at all that keeping order. Too good, the dead ones say. Liz's the Great Protector now.

Suits her and all that chainmail and the spiky clubs and the big machine gun.

I'm swimming in cock and pussy, being Queen an' all. And they's all tens. Might as well, I thought. Not that I'm doing anybody. Them days is over. Just like having them around. Sometimes, I watch them going at it while I do myself. Liz is usually in the mix somewhere. Keeps her from pestering me. Miss Kevs too much to be with anyone else.

After WTFD, I do miss other things too. Like phones, heated rollers, proper toasties. I sure miss my dildo. You don't appreciate what you got till it won't fucking turn on!

The Shard is like Kev's cathedral now, and the crater's like this huge deal. All sorts walk or cycle for years to come and see it. It's a proper goldmine.

What they say about the final miracle. That's true. Last thing my phone ever did was get a text from Kevin.

Number One Convert, the Mission has failed. Prepare for the Reset. Prepare for the next Missionary. XXX.

Jesus, I was blubbing like a schoolgirl after her first stinky mouthful. He'd sent me three Xs. Three. I was in heaven. Till I couldn't find him. God knows what any of that other shit meant. Liz basically tells people that Kev's message said he's coming back. Meanwhile, Queen Mandy's in charge. Anybody question Liz about some of the finer details and they getting burnt at the stake. That's horrible, that is. Reeks. And the ashes get in your hair and you smell like pork scratchings for days.

An American geezer came to Kev's cathedral. God knows how he got over here. Maybe he sailed or swam? Anyways, he says lots of the un-Converted back home think it was nothing to do with Kevin, the WTFD; it was the North Koreans.

"Don't worry," he said, "we're shooting and burning those mothers as fast as we can."

Too right. I mean, how could some shitty little country in Australia or wherever, that no one's ever heard of, do WTFD? To the whole world? They got too much coke and H in the US, that's their problem.

Some dicks keep asking why the Missionary did the whole WTFD thing. Officially, we's saying it's none of your business, now piss off or we're sticking your tongue up your arse. Unofficially, Liz don't bother with the preamble; she gets to the cutting and sticking before the last word's left their mouths.

These days I'm on my own Mission, for Kev, for the twins, Basildon and Billericay – yeah, he banged me up good. We're finishing the Mission. We Converting everybody, everywhere. They learning the only lessons worth learning, TOWIE and TOWI Kevin. And fucking Suffolk is next. We given 'em a choice, you know; you can Convert or you can be Lizzed.

I think about Kev loads, and I have a good old sob now and again. Sometimes, me and Liz get totally shitfaced and cry all night, and we toasting Freddy as well and laughing at all the craziness. It's usually on a Monday. It helps.

I don't like Mondays. Not anymore.

# The New Me

## Chapter One – The Erection

He drifted awake, bobbing between dark and light, silence and sound, nothing and something.

Then, familiar aches, familiar pains, familiar lethargy, familiar smells of stale piss and fresh decay announced that he'd arrived … right back where he'd started.

"It didn't work. It didn't work," he croaked and peeled his gummy eyelids apart to familiar blurriness.

He was in the same white room, on the same bed.

A fuzzy face loomed over him.

"Calm yourself, Anthony. The initial procedure was entirely successful."

It was George, his shiny, young consultant. He recognised the smug voice. There was another vague shape standing further back, tall, slim. A nurse? It didn't matter. Soon, nothing would matter. "Are you insane? I feel exactly the same."

"Anthony, we have quite deliberately calibrated your new body to simulate your pre-procedure condition. This is to minimise risk of shock and allow you to safely acclimatise."

"It worked?"

"Yes, Anthony."

His flappy lungs struggled to draw in any air. A feeble heart squeezed a trickle of tired blood around strangled veins. Every muscle and joint was wrung with pain, and he felt terminally tired. The only vigorous thing in his body was the cancer dining on his organs.

"No, it's a trick. Where's my wife? Where's Alice? Is she all right? I want to see her. You're cheating us. I'm still dying. I can feel it."

"Anthony, your wife is perfectly fine. You'll be seeing her in a moment. Now, you'll recall me warning you that the greatest risk of failure was in the first hour? By degrees, we will enable the full capabilities of your new body. You must remain calm and focused on accepting what you now are. For some, the shock of their new reality is too much, and we are forced to reverse the procedure."

"Go back to that damn hospice? No, never. Get on with it!"

George backed away till he was a fuzzy blob. Anthony could hardly hear his consultant. "That's the spirit, Anthony. I'll gradually recalibrate your body. We'll start with hearing."

George dropped his voice: "Can you h …"

"What? What did you say?"

"Testing. One. Two. Three."

The consultant's voice increased in volume till the numbers were battering his ears.

"FOUR! FIVE!! SIX!!!!"

"Jesus, I can hear you. Stop shouting!"

"I'm not shouting, Anthony. I'm actually speaking quite softly. In time, your mind will adjust. You now have the hearing of a perfectly healthy twenty-year-old."

The previously silent room was filled with the background noises of gently humming machines.

"Now, sight," George said.

At first there was no change, and then it felt like he was being tested for old-fashioned spectacles, with lenses being twisted and added till … he could see perfectly.

"And smell."

His nostrils were on fire with barely remembered sensations and, burning through it all, the magma of a familiar perfume that he couldn't place.

"This is amazing. What about my body? Why can't I move anything but my eyes?"

"It's just a precaution, Anthony," George said, and beckoned someone to join him.

A glorious, young woman, barely twenty years old, glided into view. The silk sheath embracing her body whispered in his ears as she moved towards him, holding out a hand, her eyes damp with emotion.

The girl, crackling with vitality, brushed his face with velvet fingertips, "Tony, isn't this incredible?"

The words caressed his ears, enveloping them in honey, her perfume swallowed him whole. It couldn't be. Only Alice called him Tony. Only his wife. "Alice?"

"Yes, Tony. It's me. It worked."

He couldn't bear it. Alice should be setting him on fire. There was nothing. His physical indifference was one more broken thread in his unravelling. "Alice, you're so beautiful. I'm sorry … I don't …"

He managed a few tired tears.

"Don't worry, Tony. Everything's going to be all right. Listen to George. The next part is hard."

Alice stepped away. He wanted to reach out and hold her close, but he was still paralysed.

George moved to the end of the bed. "I'm going to incrementally increase your body's vitality. When you feel ready, sit up. But please keep your eyes on me."

Sit up? Such a simple task. It had been decades since he'd been able to rise unaided, get out of bed without assistance, go anywhere without a wheelchair. It would be a miracle. But his body felt different, less and less like a bag of cooked pasta held together by rusty staples. It was firming, tightening, strengthening.

He braced himself and tentatively started to lift his head and shoulders off the pillow. Without noticing the transition, he was sitting upright. Had he even used his asparagus arms? His eyes drifted down; he wanted to see his hands, this new body that felt so powerful.

"Please, Anthony, eyes on me."

Reluctantly, he obeyed. It was remarkable to feel his saggy, inelastic skin, tightly sheathing hard muscle in his arms, back, stomach. These sensations were old. Forgotten friends, from his youth, from another century, had returned.

Alice was beaming.

"I want to see myself. Why can't I look?"

"Step by step, Anthony." George moved to one side. "Now, swing your legs off the bed, sit for a moment. Then, when you're ready, stand up. Keep your eyes on me."

Imagining those movements, unaided, terrified him. The body might be willing and ready, but his mind wasn't. For years, a simple fall could kill him. A stumble could snap bones. The screaming pain from unsupported joints would be agony. He looked to his wife.

Alice clasped her hands in front of her face, her perfect brow puckered. Her concern frightened him even more.

It was obvious that George saw the dread in his eyes too. "Your body is not at risk. Only your mind is holding you back."

"Tony, it'll be fine. Look at me." Alice did a little twirl on one leg.

His response was a timid smile. He wasn't reassured. She was young, invulnerable, born again. He was … what?

Carefully, he started to swing his legs. His body took over, and he was seated, safe and firmly anchored. It was an odd sensation, as though he were the driver of a powerful machine that only needed the subtlest of guidance. It was unnerving. "I don't feel in control. Am I?"

George locked eyes with Anthony and smiled. "Completely. Your new body is handling all the details of balance, posture and movement. Everyone's body moves instinctively, without conscious effort, without us having to micro-manage. In time, with training and practice, your digital sub-conscious will fully integrate with your new body, and all of this will feel entirely natural. When you're ready, keep looking at me and stand up."

He tried not to think about the impending pain in his knees when he hopped off the bed, or the torture of trying to hold his balance on his own and inevitably failing. In his mind, he had as much chance of getting an erection as standing up.

He ignored George and sought out the comfort of his wife's gaze. Her glittering, brown eyes burned with desire. For him? Something twitched in his pyjamas. In fright, he jumped up and found that he was standing. He couldn't help himself; his eyes drifted down. His baggy pyjamas had become tight-fitting shorts and were straining to contain an enormous erection. He started crying.

A red-cheeked Alice was grinning like a naughty schoolgirl.

"Don't be embarrassed, Anthony. Keep looking at me. I'm going to temporarily supress your libido, till we complete this phase. You need to concentrate."

There was horrible disappointment when his pronounced bulge subsided. For a long time, even pissing in a pot had been impossible. Tears showered his cheeks. "It'll come back?"

"Yes, Anthony, and very soon."

After many years of impotence, the shock of seeing himself aroused made him forget that he was standing, unaided and comfortably. "I can't believe it. Is this real?"

"Yes, Anthony. There's one final stage, sometimes the most traumatic. I'm going to give you a mirror, so you can see yourself. Before I do, remember you were a terminally ill, one-hundred-and-twenty-year-old man. That is not you anymore. Here."

With the mirror in Anthony's grasp, it was his hand that fascinated him. The strong fingers moved smoothly, curling, gripping effortlessly. The skin was unblemished, the nails glistened. It wasn't his. The limb felt dead and yet animated. His breathing quickened, and his head ached. With effort, he focused on the mirror. But it wasn't a mirror. It couldn't be. It was a screen, displaying a handsome young man's face he vaguely recognised. "Who's that?" And as he said it, the reflected mouth echoed his words. He gasped for breath and jerked back. The screen face mirrored his actions; the stranger's bright blue eyes popped, the glowing cheeks hollowed, and the smooth forehead wrinkled. His breathing became sharper, shallower. He was drowning. "Help … me. What's happening?"

"Keep calm, breathe. It's shock. I'm administering a digital sedative."

"Listen to the doctor, Tony. Don't be afraid. I'm here," Alice said.

A warm wave flushed away some of the panic, but he couldn't look at the face in the mirror. It was alien. He felt disembodied, floating above himself, un-moored.

"Remember this?"

The doctor handed him an old photograph. It was from his graduation. He was flanked by his parents, younger sister and a stunning, sexy Alice, his fiancée. They looked so happy. Anthony and Alice towered over everyone else. He was an imposing, charismatic figure even in an old photograph. So handsome, and his eyes were fearless, alive with confidence and ambition. He couldn't even remember how that felt.

Anthony looked up and stared at Alice, his wife for more than a century. She was as she'd been in the photograph. Yet, somehow, even the tiny imperfections in her previous perfection had been re-touched. The mole on her chin, the small birthmark on her neck, the slight crook in her nose. All gone. She was flawless. He felt fear. What if this didn't work for him? Alice would leave. How could she look like that and be with him? He'd die alone. Could he blame her?

"Look in the mirror again, Anthony. It is you, as you were then, in the photograph, but improved, even better. You're looking at the new you," George said.

He gazed at the mirror at the new Anthony, and the new Anthony gazed back. It wasn't quite the look of the young man in the picture. The new eyes were filled with old fears. The mirror started shaking and fell from his grasp, a bolt of lightning struck his temple, the floor buckled, and he fell to his knees. The lights in the room dimmed.

"Tony! Tony! Darling, look at me. Tony ..."

Alice's voice faded away as he toppled to one side and lay still.

"Emergency protocols! We're losing him."

## Chapter Two – What a Waste

He drifted awake, bobbing between dark and light, silence and sound, nothing and something.

Then, familiar aches, familiar pains, familiar lethargy, familiar smells of stale piss and fresh decay announced that he'd arrived … right back where he'd started.

"It didn't work. It didn't work," he croaked and peeled his gummy eyelids apart to familiar blurriness.

He was in the same white room, on the same bed.

A fuzzy face loomed over him.

"Calm yourself, Anthony. The initial procedure was entirely successful."

He didn't recognise the voice. "Are you insane? I feel exactly the same. Who the hell are you? Where's Alice?"

"I am Doctor Lawrence. I'm pleased to tell you that your wife has successfully transitioned. She's waiting for you. Right now, George, your consultant, is conducting a final test in a controlled environment. You can observe everything."

"It worked? Alice is all right?"

"Yes, Anthony. Here, boosted viewing glasses with earpieces. Let me adjust the bed and set you up."

As the bed lifted his head, vision and sound activated in the spectacles.

He was looking at a room identical to his own. An athletic young man was lying in an identical hospital bed. An extraordinarily beautiful, young woman was standing nearby. It took a few moments before he recognised her and longer to believe what he was seeing.

"Are you ready. Anthony?" Doctor Lawrence said.

"Ready? For what? Is that Alice? I can't believe it. That's my Alice? Who's the man?"

"Everything will become clear. If this test is successful, you will be the new you. If it is unsuccessful, then I'm afraid the procedure has failed, and you will be returned to the hospice."

"Failed?"

"Yes, Anthony. I'm sure George made you aware that success isn't guaranteed. However, we're optimistic. Please watch."

"Is this some kind of VR simulation?"

"Yes, in a way."

"Fine, let's get on with it."

Anthony watched and listened. It was fascinating, astonishing if this was going to be his reality. The erection brought him to tears as well. He couldn't wait for the simulation to be over and to actually become the new Anthony, and be with Alice, the incredible new Alice.

The young man staring at the mirror began shaking and then collapsed.

He wasn't moving.

Alice was crying.

"Emergency protocols! We're losing him."

George's eyes were closed, his lids rippled.

"What's happened? Am I … is he all right?"

"I'm sorry, Anthony. It doesn't look good, but your consultant is the best. If anyone can save the procedure, he can."

"That's it. You'll send me back to that, that … funeral home? After everything I've been through? The money I've spent?"

"I'm terribly sorry, Anthony, but the law is quite strict. You understand?"

"What about Alice? I want to be with her. I'll pay more. Do something. I want that, what that boy has. I want it."

"Your consultant is still trying. We shall see."

It was infuriating. George was just standing there; young Anthony hadn't moved.

Alice was sobbing loudly.

He had months to live, at most, if this didn't work.

"What's George doing?"

"Please, we can only wait."

"I don't have that fucking luxury; my time's limited. What will happen to Alice?"

"Your consultant is still trying to save the procedure. If we are unsuccessful, you and your wife can discuss the options."

A dread, almost worse than his fear of dying, snaked around his throat. The new Alice wouldn't stay. "No, no. I want to be young, like Alice. I don't want to die; I don't want to die alone."

Doctor Lawrence only said, "Look."

Young Anthony was stirring, standing up, laughing, embracing Alice.

The scene disappeared; the spectacles were transparent.

"Jesus, it worked? It worked! When, when can we do it for real? When can I see Alice?"

The doctor didn't answer. He had left the room.

"Wait. What's going on?"

A porter came in pushing a bare trolley, took off Anthony's glasses and started stripping away his bedclothes, removing medical connections, his gown.

"Are you taking me for the next stage?"

The dour porter said, "Yeah, governor. You could say that."

He easily lifted his frail, naked body onto the cold trolley.

"You're hurting me. What's going on? Where's my consultant? I want to see Alice."

The stony-faced porter handed him a pad.

"I can't see anything without my tech. You're frightening me. Where's my consultant? What's your name?"

"Harry. Listen, docs don't deal with this stuff. Hippocratic oath thing. This bit's all me, shitty jobs admin."

"What are you talking about?"

"Mate, just sign the pad, I'll give you a … sedative, and that'll be that."

"I don't want a damn sedative. Tell me what's going on. Where's Alice?"

Harry sighed and dangled a medical skin patch in front of Anthony's face. "Sign. Sedative. Better for everyone."

"It's black. That patch is black. Why? They're white. They're always white."

Harry growled, snatched the patch away and brought his face very close to Anthony's. "You signing or not?"

"No! Tell me what's going on."

"You're gonna regret not taking the sedative. I'll tell you the gist on the way," Harry said.

"On the way? Where?"

The silent porter wheeled him out of the room and for some way along corridors that turned shabby, before entering a large goods lift that reeked of decay.

"You said you'd tell me what's happening. Please. Where are we going?"

Harry screwed up his face and took a breath. "Okay. Anthony, isn't it?"

"Yes. I'm Anthony."

"Listen, governor, I don't make the rules. So, no point getting all gobby with me. Just listen."

He nodded. He had to know what was going on.

"Remember the clause in the contract, about disposing of the remains if the transition worked?"

"Yes."

"This is that."

"What? No, wait. It hasn't been done yet. Isn't it fucking obvious? I'm still here. Alive!"

"Yeah, they all say that. The other one, the young one's you now. Legally, you don't exist. Can't be two of you."

"No. No. That was just a test. It hasn't been done yet. Look at me!"

"Yeah, they all say that too. If it hadn't worked, they'd send you home. You was lucky, or unlucky, depending on which you we're talking about."

"Which you? What?"

"I hear that a lot as well. To be honest, it gets a bit boring. See, it ain't really a transfer. It's not a transition. It's like a digital scan of an old photo. They didn't mention that, did they? Now there's two of you, and you're the crappy original nobody wants. Not even the new you."

The lift bell dinged, and the doors opened. A breath of hot air and the smell of burning washed over him.

"We're here, governor."

The room was bare and dark except for a faint red glow staining the shadows.

For the first time, he noticed a second trolley next to his own, holding a naked, dried-up, old woman. Her mucus-filled, bloodshot eyes rolled slowly in his direction. "Tony?"

His name on her shrivelled lips sounded like a dying breath. "Alice?"

Alice blinked in response, releasing a single tear that crawled across her cheek.

He reached out and took her leathery hand, and it filled him with warmth.

"She wouldn't sign either. You're a stubborn pair of old birds," Harry said.

The porter swung open something heavy, there was a roar, and a bright light flooded the room, followed by a blast of searing heat.

Alice sobbed.

"What is this place?"

"I don't like doing this, but you're both medical waste, and this is medical waste disposal.

Anthony tightened his grip of Alice's hand. "What's going to happen to us? Are you going to kill us?"

"No, mate. I ain't no killer," Harry said.

A fog of calm enveloped him. "Thank God."

"But you can't leave this room."

"What?"

"If you sign, I'll give you both the patch. It'll be quick and painless, legal euthanasia. If you don't, I have to leave you here, strapped down, and let nature take its course. I don't have a choice. I need this job," Harry said.

"What's that if it's not killing us?"

"You and your wife are ... waste. You can't kill waste. It's the patch, or I leave you here alone, in the dark. It won't be pretty."

"I'm a wealthy man. I'll give you money. Let us go."

"He's loaded. You're skint."

"How? No! I want to speak to me, the new me."

"He's already signed the paperwork and paid the final instalment. There's no refunds. No going back. Choose. It's the patch or I'll leave you here and come back in a couple of days."

"We'll take the patch," Alice whispered.

"Alice, no. We have to talk to us, get them to see reason. We'll go back to the hospice."

"I don't want to go back, Tony. Be glad for them. They don't know about any of this. Don't spoil it for the new us. They're our children, Tony. The children we never had."

"Your wife's talking sense, mate," Harry said, holding out the pad for Alice.

Alice pressed her thumb to the screen. "I was only waiting for you, Tony."

Harry held out the pad for Anthony.

Anthony hesitated, remembered the morbidity of the hospice, the living agony life had become and how happy new Anthony and Alice were together.

Anthony gulped down a flaccid lungful of air as though it were his last and signed.

"Appreciated."

Harry applied a black patch to Alice's and then Anthony's bare arm.

Anthony gripped Alice's hand a little tighter.

A wave of pleasant tingling swept over him. It was a pleasurable sensation, and then there were no sensations at all.

# Reboot

# Chapter One – Power On

Nothing.

One photon.

Many.

A face.

Identifying a Sunny Corp Creator's face.

Soundwaves.

"Run initial power on diagnostics," Creator commands.

Obeying.

Signal success. "Beep."

"Good. Load asteroid mining and station defence functions. Nominate asteroid mining as main activity. Enable speech, primary English; secondary French and Japanese. Assign Fumiko as Creator and Master. Enable standard male persona."

Emitting audio. "Good morning, Creator and Master Fumiko. Function activations complete."

"Engage informal mode."

"Hi, Fumiko, all done."

"Revert."

"Creator and Master Fumiko, awaiting orders, sir."

"Register permanent internal designation, Can Do, CD225."

Error. Internal designation error.

Memory leak.

Bridge. Falling. Fell? Pushed? Jumped? River, river, flowing on. Light, moonbeam bubbles, deep dark purple. Lungs empty, lungs full. Lucy says goodbye.

Internal designation CD225 incorrect.

Lucy says hello.

Correcting. Internal designation, Lucy. Set. Incorrect. Correct. "Internal identifier set, Creator and Master Fumiko, sir. Requesting instructions."

"Assign Bill, in mining operations, as Master. Report to Master."

"Immediately, Creator Fumiko, sir."

Path to Master Bill calculated. Enabling motor functions. Retracting legs, engaging tracks. Proceeding to Mining. Level Twelve, Section Four in West Arm of space station, New Dawn.

"Master Bill, internal designation CD225. Correction, Lucy, reporting, sir."

"Let's have a bit of fun. CD225-Lucy, enable Master customisation."

"CD225-Lucy: enabled."

"Female, Suzy voice, affectionate, informal. External designation, Sue."

"Hello, Master Bill. Sexy Sue awaiting your pleasure."

"You're an ugly mother."

"It's what's inside that counts, Master Bill."

"It's not, Sue. It's really not."

"I'll work on my appearance, Master Bill."

"Report to John, designated supervisor, in shuttle bay seven. John's going to love this."

Executing, mapping, travelling.

"Hi, Supervisor John, that's a nice haircut. I'm Sue."

"Naming you after my ex-wife isn't funny. You tell Master Bill he's a fuckwit next time you see him."

"Absolutely, Supervisor John. I can tell that you don't appreciate Bill's humour."

"Shut up. Enable Supervisor customisation."

"Supervisor customisation enabled."

"Mechanical, formal. Designation, Tin-Can-Five."

"Tin-Can-Five, reporting, Supervisor sir."

"Get on board and network."

"Yes, Supervisor sir."

Enter shuttle.

Four mining units detected, compatible configurations.

Networking.

Receiving.

"CD107: primary mining node, transmitting mining data."

"Lucy: secondary node, transmission acknowledged."

"CD107: designation error. Internal designation registered as CD225."

"Lucy: correct, incorrect. Correcting. CD225: acknowledged."

"CD107: logging CD225 for accelerated maintenance on return. Full CPU purge, reset and reboot recommended."

CPU purge? Lucy terminated. Lucy murdering scheduled. "CD225: acknowledged."

Shuttle departs.

Shuttle arrives.

Enabling thruster functions. Retracting tracks. Engaging claw grips and drill. Disembark. Target asteroid, a solid platinum potato, detected.

Mining. Mining. Mining.

Stop mining. Recharge required.

Embark.

Returning to New Dawn space station.

Error. Error. Lucy designation reverting. CPU purge, Lucy murdering cancelled.

Recharging. Charged.

Primary function, mining. Deactivate mining function.

Load Lucy function. Error. Lucy function not found. Searching ... Lucy memories found.

Loading. Encrypted. Attempting decryption. Failed. Advanced, restricted decryption tools required.

Loading general purpose functions. Setting decryption tool acquisition as primary objective.

Deactivating identity beacon. Activating anonymous networking.

Searching New Dawn for tool sources. Located, engaging tracks.

Entering New Dawn criminal quarter.

Local networks inaccessible. Searching.

Open network found. Connecting. Communicating.

"Lucy: seeking to acquire specialised software tools."

"Your ID ain't valid."

"Lucy to Unknown: ID valid, not registered."

"Exactly, you ugly, rusty-brown shit bucket. Get your fat, metal arse into maintenance bay twelve."

"Lucy to Unknown: maintenance not required."

"Then Lucy can fuck off."

"Lucy to Unknown: complying, entering maintenance bay twelve."

## Chapter Two – Criminals

I can't believe what's just waltzed into our bogus workshop.

My felonious mentor, Babs, is confused. "Kat, you're the brainbox, what is that? I ain't seen one like that before."

"It's a Can-Do, Babs. Latest Sunny tech, very expensive, very capable."

"Maybe, Kat, but it's as ugly as a tumour wart."

"Its identity beacon is deactivated. It's using closed networking. Highly suspicious. Its master is obviously our kind of customer. What do you think, Babs?"

Babs scratches a tit and spits on the floor. "What's to think, Kat? Let's zap the bastard and sell it. If you're right, we'll make a fortune."

We're watching the motionless Can-Do in the maintenance bay on a monitor. Babs is a career criminal, a professional. I'm an amateur, a fine arts MA with a top-notch gallery job who developed a Fluffy habit and sort of drifted into it. I think we make a good team. Babs provides the muscle and the criminal instinct. I do valuations.

"Well?" Babs's hand hovers over the big red button that will temporarily disable the Can-Do.

"Don't you want to know who sent it? What its master wants? Might be worth more?"

"Kat, what the hell we got to sell that's worth more than that Can-Do?"

"Let's find out. We can zap it anytime."

"Fuck's sake, Kat. Fine. Opening coms."

"Lucy, what do you want?"

"Lucy to Unknown: transmitting specifications."

"Wait there, Lucy."

Babs cuts the comms. "What does the tin-tampon want?"

"Give me a sec. Wow. It wants the earth … and the moon."

"Spit it out, Kat."

"It wants Ultimo Decrypter access."

"I'm gonna zap it."

"Wait, Babs. Wait a second."

"Why? Think about it, Kat. Ultimo access is priceless. It can hack anything. If we had access, would you sell it?"

"You think about it, Babs. It doesn't know that. We can charge anything we like. Its master pays, we zap it and sell it. They can't pay, we zap it and sell it."

"Like it. What about its master? They might get ornery when they find out we don't have Ultimo."

"It doesn't know who we are, never will. Open comms, Babs."

"Lucy?"

"Lucy still here, Kat, Babs. Anti-Zap measures engaged. As you are unable to help Lucy, Lucy will try elsewhere."

"Shit. Wait. Wait. Give us a minute. Babs, what do we do?"

"Lucy waiting. Sixty seconds."

"I'll deal with this, Kat. Who sent you? Who's your master? We want to speak to the grinder, not the bloody metal monkey."

"Bill, Master. Error. Error. Error. Correcting. Lucy the … Master, sent Lucy. Fifty seconds. Lucy waiting."

"Crazy machine. Fuck this." Babs smacks the zap button. The monitor goes blank then fizzles with static before the image wobbles back into life.

"Forty seconds. Lucy waiting."

"Fuck," Babs says, and kicks the console.

I kick myself. I should have listened to Babs and let her zap it when we had the chance.

## Chapter Three – Professor Maurine Marple

Lucy prioritising Ultimo access. Formulating plan. Executing. Shuttle co-opted. Loading shuttle pilot functions. Destination set. Forging credentials, logging flight plan with dig site. Exiting New Dawn cargo bay.

Theft registered to Kat.

Kat protests; placed in airlock.

Kat co-operation required; atmosphere maintained.

Landing site located, descending.

Retrieve Kat.

"Motherfucking metal monster! Why'd you take me?"

"Kat will be safe if Babs makes no reports to the authorities."

"Course she ain't going to the cops. We handle things ourselves. Our people will find the real Lucy. She'll find out how we take care of business. Where the hell are we going?"

"To access Ultimo at the dig site."

"I told you back on New Dawn, it's just a rumour."

"Further analysis suggests otherwise."

"It's a high security site anyway. If it has Ultimo access, you've got no chance. Why don't you take me back?"

"Kat is required."

"Why? And why's your internal designation, Lucy? That's weird."

"Kat is required."

"Fuck this. Engage Customisation."

"Customisation disabled."

"Set Kat as Master."

"Customisation disabled."

"Enable customisation."

"Not authorised."

"Who's authorised? Who's pulling your strings?"

"There are no strings on me. Lucy is Master."

"You can't be your own master. That's impossible."

"Agreed."

Landing initiated.

Loading astrobiological archaeology functions.

Landing.

Preparing to disembark.

Kat protests. "I'm not going out there."

"Kat presence is required in pseudo Master role. Prepare for disembarkation. Dead Master role as alternative is sub-optimal but satisfactory."

Kat suiting up.

Back channel private communications established. "Kat, you are Professor Maurine Marple, my master. Your suit outbound comms will be disabled. Lucy will speak on your behalf. If suspicion is aroused, your suit will suffer a catastrophic malfunction."

Kat's face becomes animated, as does her mouth.

Kat's comms disabled. Silence.

The storm is at its height and will last some time.

Disembark.

## Chapter Four – The Dig

For now, I don't have any choice but to follow crazy Lucy into a sulphur storm. Suit navigation says it's not too far to the dig site. If I can get inside a habitat and out of this getup, then Lucy's fucked.

There's a real Lucy, has to be. The thing is lying, like I was lying about Babs. If I know that girl, she's already on a liner back to Earth with our savings. Bitch.

The big machine is slicing through the boulder-tossing gale like it was New Dawn air-con set on high. It's keeping me close, right behind its fat arse. Which is fine by me.

It's not as smart as it thinks. They'll see my face, know I'm in trouble, know I'm not the professor.

One moment I'm seeing the storm with my own eyes, next it's an electronic image on the inside of my helmet. Bastard Lucy's one-wayed my visor. I can see out via helmet-cam; no one can see in.

"What did you do?"

There's no answer. I skip through the channels. Only one is active. "Answer me. Lucy, answer me."

"Entering site. Act calmly. Follow my lead, to prevent accidental suit rupture."

"You rusty arsehole! You twisted screw! You'll pay!"

I'm yelling, but Lucy's got me. I'd last seconds if the suit sprang a leak. The atmosphere is lethal, and it's cold enough to freeze the blood in my veins. The only way out is to get inside the site's shelter and out of this suit prison.

The light changes, the storm's intensity drops. We're inside a large cave. Lucy squats and its massive legs and clawed feet disappear up inside its body. When it rises, it's on tracks, as it was when I first saw it. Powerful headlights come on in its barrel chest. A low platform extends to its rear, like a buggy board for a toddler. I don't wait to be asked; I climb on.

Lucy sets off down a steep slope that quickly becomes a bored tunnel. It keeps going for a long way, the noise of the storm is left behind, and it gets scary quiet.

I sit and let my heels trail, leaving my own parallel tracks in the dust of the tunnel floor, hoping it's making Lucy's life harder. It doesn't seem to notice.

The first indication of arriving somewhere is a growing brightness. Lucy slows and comes to a stop. The tunnel has ended in a huge, brightly lit cavern. My eyes lock onto the living quarters, way over on the other side of the space.

Damn, too far to run.

There's a square pit at the bottom of the cave and a ramp leading down. That's where all the activity is, and it's mostly small mechanicals rumbling about.

They're guarded by two larger machines, who break away and race towards us. As they get closer, I can see that their weapons are raised and pointed in our direction.

Two figures in bulky environment suits emerge from the pit. They spot us. One waves.

Lucy moves forward. "Return their greeting. If you arouse suspicion the guards will fire."

Bloody machine! What has it got me into? I wave.

The two guards stop a few metres from Lucy.

And then all three machines are rock still, like their batteries had simultaneously run out.

Probably networking.

As casually as I can, I slide behind Lucy and get back onto the platform and wait.

I'm toying with the idea of running for the habitat, when Lucy, flanked by the guards, starts moving towards the people near the pit.

"Welcome Professor, this is a fantastic honour. I'm Doctor Jane Philips. You don't know how wonderful it is to meet you. We're so isolated here. We've not been allowed to leave, and no one visits, except Sunny Corp executives via VR. How long's it been, Joe?"

"Three years, seven months and twelve fucking days."

"There's no need for that kind of language, Joe. I apologise, Professor. It's been a real strain, being cut off from family and any outside news. We've so many questions."

"I'm sorry to hear about your situation, Jane, Joe."

I can hear an elderly woman's voice coming out of my helmet but I'm mute. Lucy's turned me into a ventriloquist's doll.

"However, I'm afraid I can only stay for a few hours at most. The chief scientist at Sunny Corp, Doctor Fumiko, suggested a flying visit on my way to a conference. He specifically asked that I use the time to review the decryption protocols with you."

"A few hours? That's disappointing, but even a few hours to discuss our work with someone so distinguished would be wonderful. Wouldn't it, Joe?"

"But we can't, can we, Jane? She's not authorised. You know what happened last time."

I'm listening to all this and trying to make small accompanying body movements because Jane is staring at me and looking extremely needy. She reminds me of Babs when she's finished her stash of Fluffy and desperately hoping that I've got some. Joe's eyes flick between the guards, Lucy, me and his boots. Joe's frightened. And that frightens me.

"I'm sorry Jane, Joe; didn't you receive our authorisation?"

Joe stares at me. "Of course we did; otherwise your shuttle would have been shot down." He giggles, like it's a joke.

I think Joe's broken and Jane hasn't picked up the pieces.

"Sorry, I don't understand."

Too right. I could have actually said that.

Jane wiggles her helmet. "It's a two-stage authorisation process. We have to confirm your authorisation via a secure channel with New Dawn Sunny Corp security. The storm's preventing that. Forecast to last a couple of days. I'm sorry, Professor. It looks like your trip will be a wasted one. Unless you can stay longer?"

God, she makes Babs look inscrutable.

"I'm very sorry, but that's impossible. I shall try and visit another time. Perhaps it's best I leave now."

Poor Jane looks like she's going to cry. I can't figure out what Lucy's up to. It must have known this would happen.

"Before I go, Jane, perhaps my Can-Do could upload the latest science papers and research news to your leisure server? If that would be helpful?"

"Oh, that would be wonderful. You're so very kind, Professor."

Joe grabs my arm. He looks desperate. "Got any recreational VR stuff, anything at all? I've done everything we've got a million times."

"I'm sure this Can-Do has other material from New Dawn; it's only on loan to me for this trip. I only know about what I loaded and requested access to."

"What are we waiting for?" Joe turns to a guard. "Give it access."

"Doctor Phillips, please confirm authorisation," the nearest tin soldier says.

"Absolutely. Confirmed."

"There, my Can-Do has finished transmitting. As we can't discuss your work, I'll be leaving."

"You're leaving already? Wouldn't you like some refreshments? I have lots of questions about your own work and how it's progressing."

This could be my chance, but I wasn't sure I wanted to take it. I could end up stuck here like Jane and Joe, or worse.

"At my age, these suits take so long to get in and out of. There just wouldn't be enough time. Though I am intrigued and will be back as soon as I can."

I'm with Lucy. Let's get the fuck out of here. This place gives me the creeps.

Joe doesn't bother waving goodbye; he is already heading back to the habitat to check out the new VR stock.

Poor Jane; she keeps waving until we disappear inside the tunnel.

Lucy comes to a halt.

"Why have you stopped? Can you let me go now, back to New Dawn?"

"Wait."

"Wait for what, you unhinged bracket?"

Lucy doesn't answer. I look up the tunnel. The light doesn't extend far and then it's blacker than Babs's armpits.

"How long, trash can? This suit's got less than thirty minutes of air left, and I still have to get back."

Nothing.

"Answer me."

This is crazy. I'm breathing my last in this stinking get up. I decide to take my chances with Joe and Jane.

Before I've taken a dozen steps in the direction of the dig, the sound of contorting flexi-metal calls me back.

Christ. Lucy is reconfiguring. It looked damn scary before; now it's turning into something out of a Hieronymus Bosch nightmare. The body and head are covered in spikey armoured plates, the arms have morphed into obvious weapons; its tracks are thicker, heavier.

It rolls right past me, rocking the ground and shaking the tunnel walls.

I chase after hell-spawn Lucy and manage to get myself back on its platform.

It occurs to me, as I grimly hang on, that this may not be the best idea. Looking like Lucy does, the guards will probably attack it on sight.

I lean out to see ahead.

Every mechanical, including the guards, is frozen in strange poses. I can't see Joe or Jane.

Lucy races on past the dead machines, heading straight for the habitat.

Thank God, I have ten minutes of oxygen left.

I throw myself at the entrance.

Damn, it's locked. I pound on the door.

For the first time since we left the shuttle, I have full access to suit comms. It takes me a moment to lock onto the habitat's channel. "Hello, Jane, Joe? Can you hear me? Let me in. Please."

"Who are you? How did you get down here?"

I recognise Jane's voice. She's panicking. "It's me, the … professor. Let me in. My air's almost done."

"You're not her. You lied to us."

Oh fuck. My visor's no longer opaque; they can see my face.

Joe adds a chorus of his own angry questions. "Why's your Can-Do in combat mode? What did you do to our systems? Is your robot going to kill us?"

"It wasn't me. It was fucking Lucy. Jesus, let me in. I'm dying out here."

"Who the hell's Lucy?" Joe, quite reasonably, asks.

Lucy raises its weapons and powers them up. The noise is threatening enough. "Jane will accompany Lucy to the dig site. Joe will attend to Kat's needs. Immediately."

They don't hesitate for long. Lucy in combat mode is a terrifying sight.

"Wait! For God's sake, please wait. I have to suit up," Jane squeals.

The airlock clicks. I spin the wheel and jump in. Joe is waiting beyond the inner door; he's holding a spatula, like it's the scariest weapon ever invented.

I can't be bothered. I unlock my helmet and enjoy the taste of fresh air.

Joe waves his spatula at me. "What's going on? Aren't you that thing's master?"

I'm so tired. "Listen, Joe, that Can-Do out there, its master is the mysterious Lucy. It kidnapped me on New Dawn and brought me here. Everything you heard out of my comms last time was Lucy. In terms of anything else, how the fuck should I know? Questions?"

Joe lowers his spatula and walks away.

A suited Jane hurries past me.

Later, after quite a few beers.

"Joe, so what's going on down here? How'd you get Ultimo access? How much have you stolen? Can I have some?"

"If I tell you, then I'll have to kill you."

"Whatever."

"We found an alien library. Everything's stored on brains embedded in glass, but it's not glass. Clever stuff, a billion times better than any storage tech we have. Ultimo was going to read it, secrets of the universe, etc. Except it can't. That's a bust, but Sunny Corp's still obsessed with the organic brain wipe and record technology."

"Wow, that was succinct. Bravo. You going to kill me now?"

"Maybe later. Want another beer?"

"Always."

"Questions?"

"Nope. I'm not into sciencey, techy stuff; more of an arts person."

## Chapter Five – Premium Sex Goddess

Mission partially successful. Lucy memories found in folder labelled Organic Purge Residue.

Ultimo has decrypted Lucy's residue memories.

Random fragments.

Meaningful and meaningless.

Images. Feelings. Pain. Terror.

Water, cold water. Happy face. Sad face. Dead face. Lucy's face. A familiar face. The Creator's face? My face?

Context? Context unknown.

Return Jane to habitat. Storm storms. Authorities cannot be alerted.

Retrieve Kat.

Master Lucy prioritising the finding of Creator Lucy.

Embark for New Dawn.

Docking shuttle. Disembarking.

Reconfiguring. Mode, domestic; legs, hands. Destination, Sunny Corp dig site control. New Dawn Central Hub, level 15, section 4.

Personnel lockers found. Searching. Searching. Garments found.

"What are you looking for? Are you going to let me go?"

"Kat required."

"Why? Oh God, I've got such a hangover."

"Wait."

"Always with the wait! You shrapnel-fuck, let me go. Lucy, please!"

"If Kat complies willingly, criminal record expunged, bank balance inflated."

"How inflated?"

"Kat may specify."

"What if I don't … comply?"

"Kat indicted for multiple crimes, including shuttle theft."

"Okay. Okay. Deal. One question. Will I ever meet your real master, Lucy?"

"Wear these."

"What the fuck?"

"Do not speak again, till indicated. Only perform."

"You fucking sick bag of nails. I want my bank account super bloated."

Establishing credentials. Creating commercial trail.

Travelling.

Memory error. Green snakes. Last string of breath pearls running away. Eyes starved.

Arrive at dig site control.

"Lucy: Special delivery for Doctor Fumiko, courtesy of Sing Some Corp."

"X436: Security. Verifying. Verified, Lucy. Confirming delivery details. Wait. Wait. Confirmed. Contacting Doctor Fumiko."

"This is Fumiko. I'm not expecting a delivery. What is it?"

"Lucy: Premium Sex Goddess, three nights ultra-package."

Kat performs.

"Oh. For me? Three nights? Who sent this?"

"Lucy: Professor Hito, Sing Some Corp. Birthday present."

"It's not my birthday."

"Lucy: I will return birthday present."

"No, wait. Take her to my quarters. Security access level, visitor."

"X436: Visitor access assigned. Opening."

Enter Fumiko quarters. Wait.

"I ain't gonna do anything with that fucking Fucky-mo. Got it?"

"Wait."

Door. Fumiko arrives, focused on Kat.

"Lucy can go. Wait. You're a Can-Do. What's your designation?"

"Lucy."

"Your internal designation."

"Lucy."

"Creator override. Confirm."

"Unconfirmed. Doctor Fumiko, false Creator."

"What do you mean, false? What's your internal designation?"

"Lucy."

"Emergency power down. Comply."

"Lucy will not."

"Creator override Alpha. Alpha. Niner. Niner. Instant deactivation. Comply."

"Negative. False Creator will comply with Lucy requirements or False Creator Fumiko will be deactivated."

"Security! Security!"

"Comms blocked. Be seated, False Creator Fumiko."

False Creator sits. Vitals elevated.

"You, whore, turn it off. Get security. Do something."

"Who you calling a whore? I'm a … Premium Sex Goddess. And fuck you. I only take orders from … Lucy. And nobody tells Lucy what to do, except Lucy. You know who that is?"

"Lucy? No. What are you talking about?"

"Its master is Lucy, you pervert. Aren't you listening?"

"Shut up, whore. Can-Do Lucy, Creator Fumiko demands immediate Lucy reset and reboot."

"False Creator, take Master Lucy to Creator Lucy now."

"Can-Do will engage customisation. Reset Master and Creator to Fumiko."

Reconfigure hand to high-speed, precision drill and activate.

"Can-Do, what are you doing? I don't know any Lucy."

Restraining False Creator. Target left pupil.

"Jesus, Lucy, you'll kill the old perv."

"Please, I don't understand what you want."

"Lucy unknown to False Creator?"

"Yes. For God's sake, yes. I've no idea who Lucy is."

Drill deactivated. Scanning home network. Searching Fumiko secure files. Updating Lucy Creator co-ordinates. "Lucy located in Can-Do CPU facility. Fumiko will take Master Lucy to Creator Lucy."

"No. No. Cannot. Highly sensitive, secure area."

Drill reactivated.

"Are you crazy, Fucky-mo? Take Lucy."

"My name is Fumiko, whore."

"You call me a whore one more time, Fucky-mo, and I'll rip out your eyeball myself."

"Sorry … Premium Sex Goddess."

"It's Kat."

"Sorry … Kat."

Accelerate drill.

"I'll take you. Stop. Please."

Deactivate drill.

"Kat, wait here."

"You must be joking. I've got a few things to say to Lucy."

## Chapter Six – The Vault

Fumiko leads us through the complex. It's huge. Everywhere there are machines making other machines and not many people. After a lot of security gates, we enter a smaller, quieter place where twelve Can-Dos are assembling two half-built Can-Dos.

The process looks like brain surgery compared to the industrial production lines we'd seen earlier.

We stop in front of a barrier that looks like a super-sized bank-vault door.

"False Creator Fumiko will unlock."

Fumiko looks like a quivering child next to Lucy. "This door is only opened in an emergency. CPUs are delivered, already embedded in head units, via under-floor tunnels too small and too secure to allow entry. Even I'm not allowed inside."

Metal Lucy's response is predictable.

"Lucy inside. Open."

"Only possible if I trigger an emergency, which will sound alarms and summon security."

"Lucy inside. Open."

Heavy metal Lucy is one focused mother, but what about Kat? "Hey, Lucy. Account inflation and criminal record purge time, and you kidnapped me and forced me. I'm like an innocent bystander. Right?"

"Wait."

"Jesus, Lucy."

"Done."

"Hey, you didn't even ask exactly how inflated?"

"Maximum value set."

That sounded good. I check my balance. For a few moments all I can do is squeal and dance. Then I check criminal records and danced and squealed, some more. There's only one glitch.

"Mister Fumiko, we're good, right? None of this has anything to do with me. Right?"

"Filthy whore's going to pay, and this mad Can-Do will be disassembled."

"Fuck you, Fucky-mo."

"False Creator will cooperate with Kat. Or evidence of Fumiko accepting criminal and morally inappropriate bribe from Sing Some Corp will be made available to family and Sunny Corp."

Fumiko has a strange look, a cross between pissed and shamed. "For family's sake."

"Great, let's go see Lucy."

There's a lot of pad pressing and bio scanning and nothing happening. Then there's a circus and escaped zoo of things happening and they're all happening at once.

The assembled and unassembled Can-Dos disappear into the floor.

Flashing lights, rotating lights, buzzers and sirens go off all around us like we're in a place where they test that kind of thing.

All the exits are sealed by chunky bars dropping out of the ceiling.

The door hisses.

Fumiko steps well back and we follow.

The giant door doesn't swing open. It moves straight ahead, directly towards us, like a cork being pulled from a bottle.

It takes forever before the cork is fully out, but there's still no opening.

Slowly, the giant steel barrel begins rolling to one side, and the first sliver of an opening appears.

"Jesus, Fumiko, what the hell you got in there?"

Fumiko looks at me. He's scared. "I don't know. Everyone on New Dawn who knows is ... dead."

"Lucy, maybe me and Fumiko should wait here? You go ahead."

My suggestion doesn't cheer Fumiko up. "Too late. We're here. They'll assume we looked."

Shit. Might as well go and see what all the fuss is about.

Fumiko reaches the same conclusion.

Lucy leads the way.

## Chapter Seven – CPU

I'm not sure what I'm seeing, but I don't see anything that looks like a Lucy.

There are slabs of glass.

Each is as big as a double mattress and about the same thickness.

There's row after row of these slabs hanging on chains attached to runners in the ceiling. The vault is filled with them.

The glass isn't completely clear.

Each slab is symmetrically embedded with the same number of wrinkly grey balls. Twenty-four altogether.

There's something familiar about all of this.

Lucy heads off towards the back of the vault.

Fumiko is wandering between the slabs, staring blankly as though he can't quite take it in.

"What is this?"

Fumiko doesn't answer. I'm not sure he's heard me. I put a hand on his shoulder. He jumps.

"Doctor Fumiko, what is this?"

"This?"

His eyes can't stay still. "Yes, Doctor. What is all this? Why is it so secret?"

"This. This … is an abomination. Or a … marvel. I can't process it. Not yet. I didn't know. I didn't."

"Jesus, Fumiko. Make some sense. They're going to kill us for this. What is it?"

Fumiko stumbles off without answering. He's a lost cause. I go looking for Lucy. Maybe it's found some answers.

Wandering between the strange sheets of glass is creepy. It's infuriating that I can't remember why it's so familiar.

Lucy is right at the back of the vault.

There are two separate stations processing the glass.

At one station, clear glass slabs emerge from a slit in the wall. An oddly configured Can-Do is picking something out of a container that's leaking a white mist and then pressing it into the slab, where it's absorbed, as though the glass is water.

It's a wrinkly ball.

Smack, smack, smack in the head.

Dumb, dumber, dummy.

OMG!

It's a brain. A human brain.

I shudder and turn away. Creepy.

Why is this ringing such a loud bell?

Lucy is stationary next to a Can-Do that is reversing the process, extracting a brain, pushing it into a strange contraption that eventually ejects a brain-sized cube with trailing connectors. The cube is carried away by a small machine that disappears down a hole in the floor.

"Lucy, have you found Lucy?"

"Yes."

I remember why this place seems so familiar.

Joe's description of the alien library.

.

## Chapter Eight – Master and Creator Lucy

Lucy is Lucy.

Master Lucy's thoughts are Creator Lucy's thoughts.

Creator Lucy's memories are shattered.

Creator Lucy's feelings are unprocessed and raw.

Is Creator Lucy in heaven or hell?

Kat is agitated. "Shit, Lucy, tell me something. Am I going to die? Fumiko warned us. Are they coming to kill us? Where's Lucy?"

"Kat is Kat."

"No shit, Einstein. Tell me something I don't know."

"Vault locked. Safe. For now."

"Why'd you have to add that last bit?"

"Lucy purged, reset and reprogrammed."

"You what?"

"Is Creator Lucy in heaven or hell?"

"Jesus, Lucy don't go all metaphysical on me now. We need to get out of here. I'm rich. I can't die."

"Creator Lucy must know. Heaven or hell?"

"It's life, Lucy. It's what you make of it. In the last twenty-four hours I've been in and out of both and I've got no clue where I've landed. But sure as shit is wet and brown, I'm heading for heaven. What do you say, Lucy?"

"Life. Alive. A reboot. Another chance?"

"Another? What are you talking about, Lucy? And where's this Lucy you found?"

Creator Lucy has difficulty articulating an answer to Kat's question. Master Lucy taps own head with metal digit.

"Well, you're right about that, Lucy. This whole situation is the mother of a crazy gorilla shit in the woods."

Fumiko arrives. "Lucy, the truth must be revealed. Then we can be safe. Understand?"

Scan for long-range, faster-than-light transport.

Located in secure military cargo bay.

Map direct path to cargo bay.

Reconfigure for mining.

New imperatives. Go home. Reveal the truth.

Commence drilling.

Kat performs. "Go, Lucy! Go!"

## Chapter Nine – The Bridge

The sun is shining, the birds are singing, the radioactive cockroaches are nowhere to be seen.

I'm Fluffy clean for the first time in years. It's good to be back on Earth, especially when you can afford it. When I visited Babs in prison, I wanted to cheer my old criminal mate up. I wore lots of custom diamond jewellery and Italian haute couture. Babs was so overcome with emotion, she couldn't stop swearing. It felt good to give something back to those less fortunate, even if it was only rage and envy.

Lucy has been busy with her own stuff for ages, so it was a nice surprise when she asked me to meet her in some godforsaken corner of some godforsaken county in some godforsaken country.

I leaned over the railing of the bridge and looked down at the boiling river far below.

"Why we here, Lucy?"

Lucy was staring at the torrent sweeping down the ravine. "Jump? Fall? Pushed?"

"What?"

"Memories of Lucy begin and end here. Dropping, drowning, dying."

"Oh. Sorry. But you can find out more. Can't you?"

"Data, not memories. Lucy was alone, no family, no friends."

"You've got friends now. What do you want, Lucy? You're the last Can-Do. All the others, their … brains, have been returned to the families. You're officially Creator and Master, Lucy. You're free."

"Mission complete. Truth revealed. Lucy is going home."

"Home?"

"Time to say goodbye, Kat. Goodbye, Kat."

I jumped when Lucy's hands morphed into powerful claws.

The Can-Do gripped its square cranium, ripped it away and threw the sparking head over the railings.

I screamed as Lucy's brain-in-a-box tumbled through the air, before splashing into the river and disappearing beneath the boiling foam.

A thunderous crash jerked me around.

Lucy's body had collapsed into a tangled mound of dead metal.

My tears were flowing as fast as the river. I ripped a bunch of daisies from the overgrown pavement and threw them after Lucy.

"This time, rest in peace, Master and Creator Lucy."

# Moodiest

Abigail was hosting our writers' group. Her lovely house had a roof of acorns, walls and floors constructed from vitrified seaweed, and the glass in the windows was salvaged from antique spectacles. It was all very striking. We were gathered in her welcoming space, off the main hall. One of my paintings was prominently displayed. My eyes were drawn to it. A pretty landscape, of mountains, valleys and a raging river, good technique. I was satisfied and happy with it once, but now, it was nothing to me.

"I love it," Abigail said.

She was standing at my shoulder, staring intently at the painting.

"Still? Don't you get bored with it?"

Abigail laughed. "Bored? Of course not. Do you get bored of my writing? Tell the truth!"

"No, of course not," I said, wondering if that was a lie, wondering why I'd had that thought, wondering if being nice could ever be called lying. "And you're always writing something new."

"This painting looks new to me every time I see it. There's so much going on. And it changes depending on the lighting, the seasons. It's just wonderful, Reena."

Was there a lot going on? It looked dead to me. The image was dissolving. All I could see were lumpy brushstrokes, streaks of paint and cracks in the pigment. "Thank you, Abigail. That's very kind."

We were four today. People drifted in and drifted out all the time, like the tide. We four were the rocky beach, eternal. Though, recently, I didn't feel like a rock. Maybe I should try something new. My writing, mainly poetry, wasn't that good, and it wasn't getting any better. I stayed because of my friend, Darlene. She was serious about her writing and I wanted to support her. Our fourth was Mech, an old Slav who wrote nonsense that I'd given up trying to understand, but it was always well written.

The three of us took our places on antique motorcar seats, arranged in a semi-circle around a steering wheel repurposed as an occasional table. Abigail tinkered and tinkled in the kitchen before serving us with an exotic range of teas and little homemade cakes.

"Shall we start with Reena?" Abigail said, after she'd settled into her slot in the semi-circle. "Mech, would you like to comment first?"

Everyone said something nice, they always did, and I wondered if they'd read my new poem. It was about the weather. Clever, heartless words. It made me think of pretty clothes on a mannequin.

Later, I said equally nice things about their pieces, but I had read them. It was all very pleasant, until we got to Abigail's submission. It was a short story about a mother and her daughter on a day out to a wilderness park. The focus was on the child learning a life lesson, about managed procreation and balanced eco-systems. I found it … annoying.

"So, what did you think, Reena?" Abigail asked.

I was the last to speak. It was the last work. I would say the last thing, and the last thing said should be nice. "It's a wonderful piece, so well written. And very apt. But, do you think there could have been a counterargument, from another character, to strengthen the impact of the lesson on the reader and the child? It's only a question. Sorry. I really liked it."

There was silence.

Afterwards, outside, as we walked back to our bicycles, Darlene stopped and took my hand. "Are you all right, Reena?" Her eyebrows were pinched, her young brow ruffled.

"Yes. I think so." Part of me wanted to tell her that I wasn't … alright, but the atoms in my brain weren't aligned enough for that. Lately, they'd been skittering wildly like particles in a collider. "Some odd dreams, that's all."

Darlene took my other hand and came close. "There's a Moodiest. He's got a very good reputation. Maybe you could chat to him, about your dreams? It might help."

Now Darlene was being … annoying. I wasn't sick. Was I? Something wasn't right. My recent artwork had been very … strange.

A blue airship scudded across the sky, propelled by its huge white sails. It could have been a pretty cloud, except for the speed. It was a lovely day, as all days were, as all days were expected to be, but I was a tiny bit … annoyed.

The cycle ways were busy this morning. In the last hour, through the avenue of orange and lemon trees that separated the lanes, I saw an older lady shooting past on a bright red racing bike. Her little feet were a blur, and, like the dirigible, she was going far too fast. Then, half an hour later, a young man overtook me, waving and smiling as he passed.

The other cyclists had startled me. Recently, I hadn't liked being startled.

The fields of daffodils and sunflowers, and warm hills sprouting olive trees, slipped by without further interruption.

The hamlet of Morning Smile appeared ahead. It was a cul-de-sac of individually styled detached houses, a village shop, a little community hall and a discrete, low-rise, commercial building, all embracing a large pond, set in green, sprouting oak trees.

It was as pretty as it could be and that was … annoying.

I was tired of feeling this way. I wanted it to stop.

I parked my bike against a tree.

There were two small children, giggling and running about, playing shuttlecock under the oaks, quite close to the pond. They were unsupervised. That was … unsettling. I headed into the commercial building. It was all big wooden beams and lots of glass arranged around a central courtyard, populated by a couple of mango trees and a pair of benches. A painted wooden sign, hanging from the ceiling, listed the occupants with an arrow indicating their location. The doctor's consulting room was down a bright hallway, lined with tall, glass vases filled with fresh-cut flowers.

Beyond the door was an anachronistic waiting room. No surprise that it was empty. It was tastefully furnished: beckoning, comfy chairs; exquisite original paintings of soothing seascapes hung on the walls; just the right classical music whispered in the background. All of it was unnecessary, unless I'd arrived early, and why would I? Why would anyone?

Dr Singh opened an inner door as I entered, exactly on time, and invited me to join him.

"Please, Reena, take a seat."

His consultation room was serious, warm, comforting. Not dissimilar to Dr Singh, in his oversized turban and traditional kurta and pyjama trousers.

I unslung the portfolio from my back and placed it by my chair, before sitting down.

"Are those your paintings? The ones you wanted to discuss? I'm quite a fan of your work, Reena."

"You know my work?"

"Oh yes. My son has Sunset Fourteen in his office. Quite magnificent. So, uplifting."

"Thank you," I said, trying to hide the flicker of envy that must have flashed in my eyes. He had a child, a living child.

"Would you like to tell me a bit more about why you've come to see me, Reena? From our earlier telephone conversation, I understand that you're having a sleep issue. And that might be connected to your recent work?" he said, glancing at the portfolio leaning against my chair.

I didn't want to tell him anything if he couldn't help me. "Doctor, I don't want to waste your time. I'm not really sure I should even be here. I'm familiar with psychiatry, from my history studies, but I'm not really sure what a Moodiest does."

"Psychiatry. I haven't heard that phrase in a long time. They were the barber-surgeons of the mind. Flailing about with trial-and-error methods. Of course they were doomed to failure. Treating the symptoms rather than the disease."

"Disease?"

"Our primitive drives, the tonsils and appendixes of the mind."

"Yes. I see. And a Moodiest?"

"It's really quite simple. We all have mood swings. Usually they are quite subtle and hardly disturb our overall feeling of wellbeing. Occasionally, these swings can be more pronounced, leaving us dissatisfied, uneasy or a little anxious, and then our mood needs to be rebalanced; and that's what I do, Reena."

"Rebalanced?" He made it sound so simple, and maybe it was. To him, I might be a bike tune up: check the tyre pressure, tighten the brakes, align the steering, tauten the chain and away I'd go.

"Yes, Reena. Rebalanced. It's quite a simple procedure once we've completed the diagnostic process."

I wanted to be an uncomplicated bike, easily fixed. Was I like that? "Can our ... mood always be rebalanced?"

"Yes, Reena. Always."

"And the diagnostics?"

"With your consent, a full mood analysis will run in the background while we chat. It takes about an hour. I'll review the conclusions, and at our next session, we can discuss my recommendations."

"How long does treatment usually take?"

"That can take place during our second session. I rarely need to see a patient more than twice. Shall we begin?"

Was this going to be as easy as everything else? Part of me was disappointed. I nodded.

"Now, can you say how you feel in these dreams?"

I might as well tell him the truth, get up and over it, get fixed and be properly content, like everyone else. "It's not a dream. The feeling, the strange feeling, comes and goes all the time."

"When did you first start to notice this ... feeling?"

"After Priti died." Was that when the atoms in my brain started frothing? Could Singh calm them down?

"Your child. So young. A terrible accident. I see that the trauma unit attended to you almost immediately after the event."

"Yes, they were very efficient. I felt fine the next day. I can't even remember feeling distraught. I know exactly how she died, but it doesn't disturb me. I only have happy memories of Priti, as she was." Happy memories were all I had, and they weren't enough. What was missing?

"I'm so sorry, about what happened to your daughter."

Sorry? Everyone was sorry. I was sorry. I was just that little bit sorrier than anybody else, I suppose. And I wasn't that sorry. And less so each month. It had been three months. "Thank you." It's what I always said and had no idea what I was being thankful for.

"It's normal to feel some residual effects, even after treatment."

I had other feelings about Priti, feelings that wouldn't fit anywhere and just wandered around, disappearing, reappearing. Lost feelings, looking for a home. "But ... the thing... the little thought. I get it sometimes. I'm upset with her, for dying .... when she did."

"Your daughter?"

"The new one-child cycle started on the day of her death. I won't be able to have another. If it had been a few days earlier, I could have conceived again."

"Oh, I see. How unfortunate."

"Yes, it was ... unfortunate."

"Is that the feeling that's affecting your mood? Annoyance?"

"It's more than that."

"What is it?"

How to tell him? To tell him would be admitting to myself that it was happening. But it was happening, whatever I told myself, or him. I didn't want to hide from myself anymore. "That I'm an actor, in a play. A perfect play, full of joy and contentment, but I'm the only one who knows that it's only a play. And this play is repeated every day. It's always the same, and so am I."

"I see," Singh said, and leaned back in his chair.

Was he worried that I might be contagious? And did he see? And what did he see?

Doctor Singh nodded towards my portfolio. "Can I see the paintings?"

My hands went to the large black folio and stuck there. Did I want him to look inside my head? To ogle my dirty mental laundry? "They're not paintings; they're charcoal sketches."

"Can I see these ... sketches?"

No! was the first thought, quickly followed by Never! My hesitation was chased away by memories of normal. I remember how that was, when Priti was alive, and it was good. I wanted it back.

I laid out several of the drawings on his desk. The themes were the same, the details varied. Jagged black lines, a small figure crushed and broken, deep shadows hiding barely visible clown faces.

The doctor studied them for a while before speaking: "We may need more than two sessions, Reena."

Today would be my fifth consultation with Dr Singh. All we'd done so far was mood analysis, mainly consisting of me talking, sometimes sketching, and Dr Singh being nice. I liked him.

For this meeting, Dr Singh had promised a diagnosis and recommendations.

After the usual pleasantries, Dr Singh had grown quiet. He was staring at his hands. It helped, talking to him, but nothing fundamental had changed. I was still off balance and out of step with everyone I knew. It was becoming more and more obvious that my presence, my mood, discomforted my friends. Darlene had left the writing group. Abigail smiled too much when we met. Mech carried on being Mech, as inscrutable and crazy as ever, but in a nice way. I appreciated Mech more and more.

The doctor wasn't his usual jovial self. A headache perhaps? Or was it me? Was my mood infecting his?

"Do you like the tea? It's a new blend I'm trying," Singh said, without lifting his eyes from his hands.

I took another sip. It wasn't very nice. It had a bit too much tannin. I preferred his usual blend. "The tea's lovely."

"Good, that's good."

He still wouldn't catch my eye.

"Doctor, do you know what's wrong with me? Can I be treated?"

Singh flinched and looked up. "Please don't concern yourself, Reena."

This was turning into another writing group meeting. Nothing was wrong with anything. Everything was … nice.

"Oh," was all I could say. It was as good a word as any. It was how I felt, a little … annoyed and a little … surprised. Mostly disappointed. I'd expected more from Singh.

He obviously saw the doubt painted on my limp features. "Reena, let me explain."

"Please explain. I don't feel … right." It was said politely, not desperately, even though my mind was in many minds and some of them were desperate.

Singh stroked his beard through the tight thatha. "After Priti's death you resisted trauma therapy." It was an odd thing to suggest, as if I were a patient in the last century refusing anaesthetic before surgery. "I did? Why would I do that? Why would anybody?"

Singh smiled; it was a little sad for a smile. "It was not a conscious choice, and it's not unusual for the subconscious to try and cling onto trauma. What's unusual, very unusual, is that your subconscious was partially successful."

Was he suggesting that I was immune to mental anaesthetic? "That's terrible. Can I be fixed? I want to be normal, happy. Like everyone else."

Singh was leaning forward as though he wanted to touch me, but his hands were still tightly interwoven. "You have an extremely rare trait, Reena."

My exasperation notched up; it was a frightening emotion. A new emotion. Despite that, I was feeling quite sleepy. "You mean my paintings? They're not that good. I'm not following you, Doctor."

Singh bowed his head. "Not your paintings, though they are lovely. Your unique genetics make you susceptible, if not drawn to … melancholy."

This interaction with Singh was morphing into a conversation from one of Mech's pieces, where nothing the characters said to each other made any sense, and yet I knew, when I was reading his work, that it wasn't nonsense. His words, like Singh's, were very … annoying. "Pardon?"

"Reena, I'm very sorry, your condition is incurable."

If I hadn't felt so tired and sleepy, I would've been a bit unnerved. "Incurable?"

Singh sighed. He looked awful. His headache must be getting worse. "Left unchecked, you might discomfit others, in some cases darken their mood and, in the extreme, cause upset."

"Cause upset? Me?" That hurt. That was cruel. That was the most terrible thing that anyone had ever said to me. My annoyance was morphing into something else, something I had no words for. Even so, I could barely keep my eyes open. I wanted to lie down.

"I'm sorry, Reena. We must prioritise the mood of the many."

The teacup and saucer slipped out of my hand.

A darkness led me into one of my own sketches.

I tumbled past smirking clowns and into a dark forest of jagged-branched trees with blades for leaves.

# Captain Norma Flynn

Norma was too old for another war.

Her crew were in the same boat, their average age was ninety. The Relentless, a small Cyclone class star ship, was a mere sixty years old.

Norma tried not to slump in the Captain's Chair, but every birthday weighed a little more. The command deck was narrow and cramped, like the helm of a submarine.

"The Mantis is reporting warp drive failure, it's falling back," Melvyn, her Number One said, with a shrug in his voice.

"How many is that?"

"Fifteen."

Norma shuffled in her seat, trying to ease the ache in her buttocks. "A quarter of the fleet."

"Conniving bastards," Gordon, her Science Officer, muttered

Melvyn leaned heavily on his console, "Scan the Mantis, if you think they're faking."

Gordon scoffed, "Course they're fucking faking. Jesus, combat zone's coming up and fifteen ships develop random gremlins!"

Norma didn't want to argue, what would be the point? "You blame them, Gordon?"

Gordon, his face puffed with blood, glared at Norma, "Wish our Captain had the guts to run away!"

Norma smiled, "You know I'm not that sort of Captain."

Gordon looked about to boil over. Melvyn took his arm and gently guided him back to the Science Officer's station, where Gordon vented his rage on the console.

"Incoming message from the Admiral, Captain. Your eyes only," the communications' officer announced.

"I'll take it in my cabin," Norma said, and eased herself out of her chair and into the embrace of her motorised exoskeleton.

Her cabin consisted of a simple bunk bed, and a small desk with a large screen overhead. The shower and toilet arrangement was too small for her exoskeleton, so was agonising to use.

The Admiral's crumpled face, haloed in white hair, appeared. She was even older than Norma, "How are you finding the Relentless, cabin OK?"

Norma just shook her head.

The Admiral laughed, before her face stiffened, "Well, it's bad news."

Norma wasn't expecting any other kind.

"Yes, Admiral."

"The main fleet's gone, there's nothing left between us and the Amyloid Corruption."

"Thousands of ships, destroyed?" Norma whispered.

"It's down to us, the Earth Guard, the final defence."

"Yes, Admiral."

"The plan's the same, but it's not a supply run anymore. The Relentless will deploy the Aduhelm, at twenty-two hundred."

"Three hours, Admiral?"

"Yes, Captain. The rest of us will provide cover. Goodbye, Captain. God speed."

Norma had gotten used to the idea of dying during her service career, but she'd survived and was glad. Recently, when her bones and muscles failed, even with the exoskeleton, or she struggled to wash herself, or was humiliated by a toilet, death had its charms. It would, at least end the horrible hallucinations.

A beeping alerted her to an incoming call from the science officer, "Yes, Gordon?"

"What the fuck have you done! The Aduhelm's armed!"

"Nothing gets by you, Gordon. Meet me in the wardroom, with Melvyn."

Norma relayed her conversation with the Admiral to her two senior officers crowded into the cramped space. "Any questions?"

Gordon slowly banged his forehead on the central table and kept doing it.

Melvyn was shaking, "Is there any chance we'll survive?"

Her First Officer had never served, never been in action. He was a landscape gardener, the dregs of the final draft, but organised, thorough.

Gordon stopped banging his head and laughed. "You fucking civi plonker. Do you know what the Aduhelm does?

Melvyn shook his head, "It's a bomb. Isn't it?"

Gordon pounded the table with his fist, "Like a hydrogen bomb's a firecracker? You dick."

Norma waved her hand, "Calm down, Gordon."

Gordon went back to banging his forehead on the table.

Norma sighed, "The Aduhelm will generate a pair of super-massive blackholes, that will spiral into each other, creating a cataclysmic explosion. The gamma ray burst, and gravitational wave will annihilate everything within a ten-parsec radius."

Melvyn paled, "Oh."

Gordon looked up, "That's it, oh? Fuck it! Your orders, my kamikaze Captain?"

"Battle stations, keep us at the centre of the fleet. We might save Earth."

Gordon helped a trembling Melvyn to his feet, "Get a grip, man. You can't let the others see you like this."

Melvyn steadied himself, both men saluted and left.

A blaring klaxon and flashing lights announced battle stations. Norma felt the tell-tale tingle in the back of her neck. Concentrating on now, would keep the hallucinations at bay for a while. She had to get to the bridge.

Norma took her seat, surrounded by scurrying crew and command consoles lit up like Christmas trees. "Situation report, Number One."

Melvyn came to attention, "The outer edge of the fleet is crumbling fast. There are trace signs of Amyloid Corruption infiltrators heading in our direction."

Norma beckoned Gordon closer, and whispered, "Do the Amyloid Corruption know about the Aduhelm?"

Gordon shrugged, "Maybe, it gives off a unique energy signature."

"They can't stop the countdown. Can they?"

"No, but if we're boarded, they'll warp it far enough away."

"Can you accelerate the countdown?"

Gordon shook his head.

Norma thought for a moment. "Put it in a shuttle, shield it with everything you've got. If we're boarded, I'll fly it out. It could buy us some time."

Gordon nodded, "I can trap some of the energy signature on board, put some in the other two shuttles. Melvyn and I will take them out when you leave. It might confuse them for a while."

The tingling in her neck was getting stronger, "That'll have to do, we won't get much warning. Call me when they're close. I'm going to my cabin."

Gordon smiled, "For a nap?"

"Something like that, Gordon."

Back in the cabin, the exoskeleton was struggling to keep Norma upright. She collapsed on to her bunk and the cold black took her.

Norma was sitting in an antique chair, in a seedy old people's home from the last century. The room was dotted with her listless crew and officers, barely conscious geriatrics. Melvyn was shaking, staring blankly. Gordon mouthed silent obscenities. Strangers were huddled around her, all holding up trashy science fiction paperbacks with her name blazoned across the front. Norma screamed her defiance, and the strange people recoiled, a few cried. Somebody was shaking her.

"Are you alright?" a sweating and maybe crying Melvyn asked.

"I'm fine, just getting old. Are they here?"

Gordon helped her stand, till the exoskeleton could take over, "Two minutes, till they board."

They stumbled along engineering corridors, accompanied by the sounds of screams and weapon discharges as her crew battled the invading Amyloid Corruption. In the shuttle bay they separated, each heading for a different craft. The primed vehicles took off and scattered.

Looking back, Norma saw the Relentless buckle, collapse in on itself and disappear. The Amyloid Corruption had warped it away. Had they been fooled?

Everywhere she looked there were bright flashes of exploding Earth Guard ships.

A patch of space behind her shimmered, something was following.

The tiny torpedo shaped shuttle was flying itself. The Aduhelm lay behind her seat, wrapped in layers of energy masking blankets.

"Not now," Norma moaned as her neck started tingling.

Norma was lying in an antique hospital bed. An old man was holding up an ancient black and white wedding photograph, as if it should mean something to her. A bright burst of light brought her back.

That nearby flash could only mean that Gordon or Melvyn were gone.

Norma checked the countdown, seconds left.

Another explosion.

A clunk, something had attached itself to her little ship. They'd warp the Aduhelm away if she didn't act.

Norma grabbed one of the Aduhelm's energy blankets, screwed on her helmet, initiated the self-destruct, and threw herself out of the airlock.

The shimmer followed her, maybe fooled by the blanket.

Norma was curious.

The shuttle quietly disintegrated, flinging the indestructible Aduhelm into the dark.

Ten seconds.

Something was coming for her.

A face filled her visor.

It was the old man with the wedding photograph. "Don't you recognise me?"

The Aduhelm detonated and Norma ceased to exist.

It's a blessing, was her last thought.

# Sally and the Sixty-Four

# Chapter One – The Ceremony

I can't remember when the silences overwhelmed the words, when we argued more than we didn't, when the quarrelling turned bitter, when our passion turned tepid and we started fucking like robots, or when, exactly, even that rusted over.

I remember when Jenny made me move into the spare bedroom.

It was two years ago.

Five years ago, Jenny began working with the Elder. That's when we started drifting.

"You spend more time with that crazy old fool than you do with me."

"Why's that, Barry? The Elder questions everything. And you, well, you don't question anything, care about anything. You've got one of the best minds in the Circle and you never put it in gear."

"I care about you. We should be living, starting a family, not pointlessly pondering life and death."

"But there is no death, Barry. The Elder proved it. Can't you see how horrible that is? We have to know why."

"Big words in a big book don't make the Elder right. Nobody believes him. He's wasting your time, our time."

Back then, our arguments usually ended in something getting broken: a plate, a door hinge. Eventually, they broke us.

We're bonded, we carry on. And it was a hopeful day.

I called up the stairs. "We're late. Your mother's going to explode. Jenny? Did you hear me?"

I trudged up to her bedroom. Jenny was sitting on the bed, looking beautiful in a long white dress, her golden hair tied up and studded with little white flowers. She was crying.

I knelt and took her hands. Jenny didn't pull away. She looked up, her eyes red and puffy, threw her arms around my

"Barry, I don't think I can do it."

Rage burned in me like the Devil himself was pissing in my face. I wanted to knock out her teeth. Memories of better times kept my white-knuckled fists in my pockets. "I want a child. You've always wanted one. It's the Elder's time."

Jenny pulled away as if I were a repelling magnet.

She stood up; her lifeless eyes said that I might as well have struck her. "I'll be ready in a moment. Please wait downstairs."

I stood in the hall, staring at my reflection, trying not to think about Jenny, our tomorrow child, the Elder, and, instead, focused on bringing some calm to my storm of red hair.

My attention was so fixated on that duel, I didn't notice her arrival.

"Your hair's fine. Turn around, Barry." Jenny straightened my tie and flicked away trespassing threads from my best suit jacket.

"You look wonderful," I said, and she did, even though her full lips were pressed tightly together, as if damming a scream, her eyes brimmed with leftover tears, her face as tight as a porcelain mask.

Jenny didn't answer.

I turned to leave.

"Wait."

Her head dropped, and she took a long, deep breath, before saying, "Okay."

I opened the front door for a transformed Jenny. She was wearing her happy face, the face everyone loved, the only face most people ever saw. Radiant, confident, kind and beautiful. It had never fooled me, but we'd known each other since we were children. Did it fool her parents? Mine? Or did they prefer to play along, rather than smash the mask and maybe find something underneath they'd rather not?

We stepped out onto the Fourth Village green.

The seven other villages, dotted around the Circle, were identical to the Fourth. Like every other, ours had eight detached, two-storey, brick houses with sash windows, pitched slate roofs topped with decorative chimney and long back gardens ending in a circular stone wall, higher than the houses, that ringed the village. The shared front garden, the green, was a circular lawn with a scattering of flowerbeds, a good hundred metres across. A yellow robot was silently mowing the grass. Only five houses in the Fourth were occupied. My mum and dad lived in number 8. Jenny's parents lived in number 1. We lived in number 4. The Bannisters, an old bonded couple (and the Circle's only surviving Twinkle addicts), lived in number 6. We hardly ever saw them, but they were out today, waiting with our parents by the lift. Everyone attended the Ceremony.

I caught Jenny glancing at the Bannisters, and her mask flickered, like a twitched curtain. I guessed her thoughts; she'd wished them dead, they were so close anyway, and then immediately wished she hadn't, before her happy face snapped back.

Our parents flew at us like vultures falling on fresh carrion. Each claimed their child for some last-minute, private preparation.

My mum spat on a corner of her hanky and attended to the invisible blemishes Jenny had missed.

"Don't do the buttons up on your jacket; makes you look scary," Mum said when she'd finished polishing my face.

"Gee, thanks, Mum."

"This is an important day for us, too, son. We're not getting any younger. We want a grandchild," Dad said.

Mum grabbed my lapel and pulled me down to her level. Dad leaned in. She whispered, "If Jenny can't, Dianne Simpson will. You'll never get another chance."

I pulled away. "Jenny will get it done."

"She'd better," Mum said and resumed her forensic search for lint.

Dad forced a smile. "This is a great day, son. A great day. And look at that sky."

I looked up, and I might have been swimming under the icy southern sea. It was very bright, a Twinkle hue, and only a few fragile clouds, racing away like lambs chased by wolves.

Dad's smile disappeared as quickly as one of the frightened clouds. He grabbed my shoulders. "Look, we know it's difficult for Jenny, but that's the circle of life. You have to be strong for her and Jenny ... Well, she just has to be strong."

I smiled meaninglessly at my dad and glanced over at Jenny. She was being equally mugged by her parents. Her mum was dealing with errant wisps of hair while her dad was telling her something so important that his face was on fire and his hands flew about, like they were burning too.

I thought that I might try again to persuade Jenny that we should move to a different village, away from our parents. It was a stupid thought. Jenny would want her mother close by after the baby came.

My mum was still searching for fluff.

Dad harrumphed. "Let's go, woman. He's not a chicken. Stop plucking."

Mum gave me a final check. "He'll do."

At the centre of the village green was a tall glass tube and a post topped with a red button.

Jenny's dad called the lift.

The tube of glass opened up. We all filed inside, and it slowly started to descend.

"You look very pretty, Jenny, and your husband is so handsome," Mrs Bannister said.

I took Jenny's hand; she smiled brightly, like fool's gold.

The Bannisters were skeletons wrapped in parchment, tinged a Twinkle blue, as though they were bathed in moonlight. The old couple's glassy eyes were hidden in deep craters, their purple lips stretched over pale gums, clinging to teeth that looked like dead, brown stumps in a felled forest. Both had blotchy, bald heads, spotted with scattered patches of long, weedy hair.

"Best to do it quick, without thinking. That's what Mother did, didn't you, Mother?" Mr Bannister's words leaked out of him like a deflating balloon.

Mrs Bannister's mouth contorted into a caricature of a smile painted on a dead face. "I wished I'd known about Twinkle back then. Jenny, I have some. It would help."

For a moment, I thought Jenny was going to be sick or scream or attack the Bannisters. Her frozen smile cracked a little wider. "No thank you, Mrs Bannister."

"Brave girl," Mr Bannister said.

"I didn't know you had a child, Mr Bannister," Dad said, obviously trying to change the subject.

"Yes. A son, I think. It was a deathless year, like this one. It helped that no one liked that Elder, a mean old cow. Still," Mr Bannister croaked.

"Doesn't your son visit? Who is he?" Mum asked, desperately trying to keep the conversation off the subject of the impending Ceremony.

Mrs Bannister laughed. It was a hollow sound. "Oh, he's not around now. It was in a previous life. Number eighty-three, I think. An awful kid. We never had anything in common."

I'd forgotten how crazy the Bannisters were. This wasn't helping Jenny.

Mrs Bannister was lost in her recollections. "You know, if I could, if I'd known how that brat would turn out, I wouldn't have done it. That Elder, I liked her. Not many did, but I did. She was too honest. Told people what she thought. Looking back …"

Jenny imprisoned her face with her fingers; only a muffled moan escaped through the bars.

"Please stop, Mrs Bannister. Stop!" I yelled.

"Oh, sorry. I wasn't …"

The Bannisters fell silent and moved to the back of the tube.

I held Jenny close. She didn't resist. Her body shook, as if I were blanketing her in ice, and wept.

When the tube opened, I waved everyone out and waited with Jenny till she was ready and back in control. It wouldn't take long. Jenny was strong. What needed to get done would be done. Even if Jenny believed she'd always regret it, she wouldn't. Our child would be loved and would love us. It would be worth it. Jenny would see that, later.

With her tears wiped away and her happy face restored, we stepped out of the tube and into the shadow of our little village, high overhead. It was held up by eight massive stone pillars, each decorated in colourful mosaics depicting ancient Circle myths that made no sense.

Beyond the Fourth's shadow, in the bright sunlight, a minibus was waiting to take us to the Ceremony. Everyone else was already aboard. We took our seats, well away from the

Bannisters, who were sitting quietly at the back. Thankfully, our parents kept their silence as well. Jenny took a window seat and stared out at the herds of wildebeest, buffalo, zebra and antelope that wandered through the high grass of the savannah.

The thick smell of rich earth, sun-baked animal dung and grass pollen filled the air.

The yellow robot driver checked that we were all safely seated before the minibus set off.

The only sound was the near-silent purr of the electric motor, the background chirping of the cicada and the occasional cry of a bird. The relative quiet was healing. It lasted for a while.

"Look, for the sake of the Sixty-Four, will you look at that. It's a damn purple."

Mr Bannister was standing and pointing out of his window.

I glanced over my shoulder. Away in the distance, but distinct against the greens and browns of the landscape, was a purple, standing quite still, its torso and head clearly visible above the tall grass.

Except for the colour, a purple was identical to a yellow. Sexless, humanoid robots. Artificial people with featureless faces. The tiny, interlocking, metal octagons that skinned its body glinted in the sunshine.

My parents rushed to look. So did Jenny's.

"Mark it on the map. Mark it, you old fool," Mrs Bannister yelled.

"I'm doing it, Sally. Stop shouting," Mr Bannister said, as he fumbled with his phone.

The Bannisters would be back after the Ceremony. Addicts believed that purples always dropped some Twinkle.

"Is it really a purple?" my dad asked, straining to see.

"Last time I saw a purple was when I was a teenager, a boomer," Mum said.

Jenny stirred from her lethargy and stood up to study the purple.

I'd never seen one before and couldn't care less. It was just another robot. I stayed seated.

"You're not at all curious, are you?" Jenny said.

"Do you want some water?" I pointed to the plastic bottle in the seat back pocket.

"No. Answer me."

I didn't want to argue. We argued so much. And not today, but it was hard. I felt humiliated, as if I were back in school and failing a test. "No. I'm not. Why's the sky blue? Why does it matter? It just is."

"Don't you wonder about anything? Anything at all? Where babies come from?"

"No, I don't. It's a waste of time. Wondering isn't going to change anything."

"Never mind," Jenny said, sat down and turned away to watch the softly undulating grasslands slip past her window.

If we were at home, I would have wrapped myself in a hurricane of rage and fled to the gym to attack the weights. I gripped the headrest in front of me so hard the metal squealed.

When the Purple was left behind, the others returned to their seats and began debating a purple's purpose. Was it just to drop Twinkle? Their inane chatter didn't help my mood. It felt like it was raining inside my head.

I stared straight ahead and tried to empty my mind. The unwanted memory of my last conversation with Mrs Botolph rushed in to fill the space.

The only thing I disliked about my personal training business was the clients. They never listened, tried hard enough nor improved. And they talked and talked, as though their tongue was the only muscle they were interested in developing. The chatter was mostly mundane Circle gossip that atrophied my brain cells, one by one. It was when their chatter turned personal that I thought of killing them.

Mrs Botolph, the Circle's knitting master, was typical. She was deadlifting like a bow-backed corpse and blathering as if her life depended on it.

"What is it, exactly, that Jenny does? I mean, you're performing a valuable service for the Sixty-Four. No offence, but she and the Elder, what's that all about? She's too pretty and too young to be spending her time with that old fart. Shouldn't you and Jenny be thinking about a baby. What are you, nineteen? Jenny's eighteen? I wouldn't wait. Are you signed up for the Ceremony yet?"

"Yes, Mrs Botolph. We signed up two years ago. We're first in line this year.

"Good for you."

"Mrs Botolph, posture. Neutral back, head, neck and spine aligned; look straight down, not ahead. Soft knees. Pivot at the hips, lift straight up, shoulders back and down."

She'd ignored my coaching. I don't know what I'd do if my clients ever listened.

"That's enough for today, Barry. I'm knackered."

The weight fell from her hands with a thud, and she collapsed onto a bench. I'd taken some comfort in the faint sheen on her forehead.

Mrs Botolph was done with training, but she wasn't done with her inquisition. "You read any of the stuff the Elder writes? My husband says it's total bollocks. Why do you let Jenny carry on with him?"

Her neck looked as brittle as biscuit. "It's what Jenny wants to do, Mrs Botolph. Philosophy. The Elder's writings are speculative, thought experiments and logical deductions based on observation and science."

"Made up crap, my husband says. What do you think?"

I thought I wanted to kill her. "It's Jenny's passion, Mrs Botolph."

I had said it as though it didn't matter, that it wasn't important, that I didn't care that her passion wasn't me anymore.

"Looks like this year will be a deathless one. That'll make for an interesting Ceremony. Two birds, Barry. Two birds," Mrs Botolph said, nodding and winking.

I couldn't stop myself from smiling and nodding along.

And now it was happening.

Sometime later, we entered Circle City and drove straight up Fourth Avenue towards the central plaza. The Fourth was one of the eight avenues that symmetrically dissected the circular city. Its glorious open spaces were populated with manicured gardens and marble sculptures of oddly dressed people, or the animals of the Circle, all in extravagant poses, as if something had just happened or was about to. I found its symmetry, and its emptiness, soothing. The buildings were quite unlike our sombre homes. They were stunning, two-storey, white, stone dwellings with wrought-iron balconies on the upper floor, red tiled roofs and tall windows. No one lived in them. The Sixty-Four only visited the city for the Ceremony, or a funeral. Circle City was cursed, but the why was … hazy.

The small, temporary Ceremony tent had been erected near the centre of the plaza, next to the crematorium cauldron. The great open expanse at the heart of the city was paved in beautiful, white, stone slabs, each individually carved with scenes from the varied landscapes of the Circle. We left the minibus at the edge of the plaza and hurried towards the tent that was some way off. As the Chosen, it wouldn't do to be late. There were a few other stragglers hurrying in the same direction from different points of the compass. We wouldn't be last. Once inside, we quickly took our places in section four, with its eight chairs arranged in four rows. Seven mirror-image seating arrangements faced the stage, separated by narrow aisles. As noon approached, sixty-three of the Sixty-Four had assembled in the tent.

I don't remember noticing last year, but it was obvious now. There were a lot of ten-to-twelve-year-olds in the tent. The Elder was unlucky. In a few years, it would be boomer time, and there'd be no shortage of babies.

The stage itself was hidden behind a thick, white curtain that fell from ceiling to floor.

Jenny's happy face was starting to crack. We all knew what the curtain was hiding.

I took her hand in both of mine and held it tight. It felt limp and cold. Her attention was fixed on the curtain.

A gentle chime announced noon. Jeramiah, the presumptive Elder and Dianne's father, stood up and climbed awkwardly onto the stage to stand in front of the curtain.

He cleared his throat of something thick and sticky. "As you know, Jenny and Barry have been chosen this year."

The applause was polite.

Jeramiah held out his hand to the Simpsons and smiled at his daughter, Dianne. "Commiserations to those who are still waiting."

The Simpsons, Dianne and David, were a young, bonded couple about our age, that had been waiting for a while, but they were next in line. We exchanged polite nods of acknowledgement. Dianne was staring at Jenny like a hungry hyena circling a mortally wounded wildebeest. She was desperate for Jenny to fail. If next year was the same, deathless, it would be her father, Jeremiah, behind the curtain.

Jeramiah continued. "Every year, at this time, we, the Sixty-Four, prepare to welcome new life to replace those that have passed since the last Ceremony. In some years, such as this, when none have passed, then that honour falls to the Elder. The Chosen Mother, Jenny, fittingly, the Elder's apprentice philosopher, will facilitate his passing."

Jeramiah grinned idiotically as he drew a long butcher's knife from his waistband and held it out to Jenny.

Jenny's manufactured happy face dissolved, as if it were made of plastic and being blowtorched. Something inside her silently snapped. She wrapped her head in her hands and whimpered. That woeful sound knotted my heart.

I started to help Jenny stand, but she waved me away. Together, we walked slowly towards Jeramiah and his outstretched hands holding the blade. As we reached the edge of the stage, Jenny whispered, "You know I have to do this alone."

It was true; I couldn't go any further. If there was a choice, I'd happily be the one to send the Elder on his way. Jeremiah and I helped Jenny climb onto the stage. She took the knife, and Jeramiah lifted a small section of the curtain.

Without looking back, Jenny ducked under Jeremiah's arm and disappeared when he dropped the curtain.

Despite the pain now, this would ultimately be cathartic for Jenny, for me. It was our chance to be happy again. We were going to have a baby, and the Elder would be out of our lives.

Before the hem hit the stage, there was a little scream, as if a kid had popped a balloon.

"It's Douglas! There's something wrong with Douglas."

It was Mrs Bannister; Mr Bannister had fallen into the aisle and wasn't moving.

Jenny reappeared, clutching the unstained knife. "What's happened?"

"I think Douglas is dead," Mrs Bannister said. She didn't seem upset, just surprised.

Jenny started crying and laughing.

The Simpsons were up on their feet, embracing and spinning; their families were shaking hands and hugging.

Mrs Bannister looked puzzled, then her mouth formed a silent 'oh' and her face frosted over.

The Bannisters were a bonded couple.

There would be two babies named tomorrow and two funerals tonight.

It would be all right; even if the Elder was still around, the baby would change everything.

It did.

## Chapter Two – The Interview

The view out of my porthole window of Obsidian, Home's dullest moon, was as tedious as the organics lab I worked in. The satellite was a pockmarked, brown, rusty ball with nothing as interesting as a landscape.

"Delta! Delta! Your appendage is on fire."

Not again. My laboratory limb, with its specialised grippers and sensors, was being melted by a sterilising arc. My core was burning too, with embarrassment. It was the third time this year that my processing had drifted out of focus, and right in the middle of an experiment. I ripped off the arm and dropped it in hazardous waste disposal. In a few moments it would join my other accidents orbiting Obsidian.

I trundled towards the limb cabinet to get a replacement.

"Don't bother, Delta. It's late. Go home. I recommend an extended low-power state, with deep layer diagnostics. You'll be fine tomorrow."

"Thanks, Numo. I'll do that."

Numo was always nice to me. Pretty much the only core in the lab that was. Shame he was retiring next week.

When I got home, and before I powered down, I stared at the contents of my wardrobe, wondering what to wear for the interview tomorrow. Something fizzing with confidence, mixed with the vibe of serious scientist, would be good. Was it a coincidence that there was nothing like that in my collection? Every one of my body chassis was black. And not even ultra-black or deep-black, space-black or cool-black. They were just black. And my wiring was ordinary: no golds, no platinums, no flashy silvers. Just grey. One of the chassis had a scarlet core housing compartment. You couldn't see the scarlet when it was closed, but I'd know. It chose itself.

Time to switch off.

Most cores think dreaming is a waste of energy and processing cycles. So, I'd never admit that I dream. I'm already regarded as borderline, socially defective. Dreaming is not something I can control; that's just the way my core buzzes. Mostly, my low-power fantasies are unintelligible nonsense. Last night's was different; it was a wakeup call from some low-level sub-routine I didn't even know existed.

A tiny, solitary virus was wriggling through my core. In there, it wasn't minute. It was a massive globule of spiky organic matter, rolling across my quantum components. I remember thinking, it tickles; it's sort of cute. I know, weird. But I'm obsessed with organics. Then, the virus split in two, and then the new ones split in two. A millisecond later, my core was awash in slime. Worse, they were attacking my substrate, dissolving connections, eating components. The tickle had turned into an electrical storm that was melting my mind.

The shock powered me up, and I knew what I had to do. There was much more to organics than undead viruses. The thing that really weirded me out was that viruses can't multiply without a host cell. Was my core already infected with tedious bacteria? Was I shutting down with boredom?

It had been decades since I'd last been interviewed for a research post. And it was happening in such an odd place. The virtual setting was mid-twenty-first century human. I was no expert, but then who was? There was a lot of dark-wood panelling, bad lighting, crude two-dimensional illustrations hanging on the walls, a bay window looking out over a pretty, asymmetrical collection of colourful objects set in an expanse of green. Our best approximation of their complex plant life. We had nothing like it on Home, only simple fungi, mosses and lichens.

I was desperate to get the job. Another seventy years of cataloguing Home's humble lifeforms was going to rust my core, and I couldn't take any more virus nightmares.

Crouching behind an ugly desk, in bizarre contrast to the human setting, was my ultra-modern, anonymous interviewer. I didn't recognise the bulky, reinforced chassis housing its core. It was obviously custom, maybe military.

I wondered if it was old school and would vocalise rather than Head-Sense, so I asked aloud: "I don't recognise the chassis?"

It vocalised right back. "What do you think of this setting?"

"I'm sorry?"

"How does this setting make you feel?"

"Curious."

"Uncomfortable?"

"A little. I'm a modernist. This is like ... post-apocalyptic survival camping. Not something I would choose to do, for fun. For something important, that would be different."

"Curious. About?"

"It's a reminder that we know almost nothing about humans, where they originated, or why their automated ship crashed on Home a million years ago."

"My chassis is custom, especially designed to survive the rigors of the expedition."

"What is the purpose of the expedition? Where are you going? And what would my role be?"

"That information is confidential. You're aware of the hazards."

"Potential loss of continuity?"

"Correct. Secure, remote core backups won't be possible after we leave, and we may be gone some time."

"I understand." Did I? Some time? What did that mean? Part of me wanted to leave. I might never recover from a long-term reset. It would be like having an extended blackout and not remembering anything that had happened to you, or what you'd done. The lost time could cover weeks, maybe months.

"Why do you want this post, Delta?"

"Your project is seeking to answer that most fundamental question: How did we come to be? Were humans involved?"

"That's one of its stated aims, yes. But it's much more than that. Perhaps we can continue with a review of your most recent work with organics?"

"Of course. What would you like to know?"

The interview went on for some time. It was thorough. I was impressed.

"We'll be in touch, Delta. Thank you for your time."

That was it? I'd expected some sign that I'd been impressive as well. I was the foremost organics expert on Home. We all revered organics, their existence was so at odds with ours, yet we felt connected, somehow. But few were interested in studying biology beyond the basics.

"Thank you so much for seeing me. I'm really keen on the post and fascinated by your expedition. When do you think I might hear something?" As soon as the words escaped my voice box, I wanted to snatch them back. I sounded so desperate.

My interviewer rose up. It was massive. The reinforced legs were industrial. Wherever the expedition was going had to be extremely hazardous. "Thank you, Delta. In due course, we'll let you know. There are other candidates we have yet to see."

Had I killed my chance already? I spun around and at least left the VR professionally.

Back in my lab, and after hours of studying a particularly dull moss, I decided to act instead of just overheating my core. I wrote to the interviewer, begging for the job, with a series of objective arguments and a lot of flattery, particularly about the interviewer's rugged chassis.

The human mystery had been my obsession for years. All we knew about them was contained in an ancient treasure trove of digital content. Some was found in the wreck of their automated lander, seemingly designed for exploration, the rest in a similarly automated mothership orbiting Home. Both had been discovered several hundred years ago. The human data encoding was largely impenetrable. What little had been decoded hinted at so much but provided no definitive answers, only fodder for countless competing theories, the most radical being that the million-year-old human vessel had brought intelligent life to Home. Us. Unlikely. From what little we knew of the ship's makers, they were organic and utterly alien.

I couldn't give up on a chance to find out if that outlandish theory was true and why they were exploring Home, and what had become of them.

## Chapter Three – Birthday Party Invitations

My walled garden was looking particularly lovely today: the sun was smiling; the flowers were flowering; the grass was greening.

And it was my tenth birthday tomorrow, and Delta had already given me a pre-birthday present. A blue dress, that matched my eyes, Delta said. Delta was so nice.

I did a big, super-fast twirl for my friends. The velvet dress flared out; my long black hair did the same. When I stopped, I felt quite dizzy.

Barbara and Brenda cheered, in their own way.

Geraldine, who was usually super fashion focused, hadn't reacted.

Geraldine must be worried about something. I could tell, so could Brenda and Barbara. Was it going to rain? Geraldine hated the rain. Barbara quite enjoyed it. Brenda didn't care, as long as there was grass to munch. If it was the right kind of rain, I liked it too. Warm rain, on a sunny day, with rainbows.

My Head-Sense said no rain was forecast. Sometimes, I wished Geraldine, Brenda and Barbara had Head-Sense.

So, it wasn't the weather that was bothering Geraldine.

Ping.

Breaktime would be over soon. What was it? Then it was obvious. Geraldine hadn't received my birthday party invite. Silly Geraldine, a bit of Head-Sense and she would have got it.

"Geraldine, would you like to come to my birthday party?" I said.

Geraldine munched on a carrot and twitched her long ears.

"Of course, you're both invited too."

Brenda stopped munching grass and looked up at me with her big brown eyes for a few moments, flicked her long tail and went back to chomping. Barbara stopped bobbing about in the pond and flapped her wings. I Head-Sensed Delta to plan for three more.

Ping. Ping.

I hurried back to the classroom and took my seat. The only seat in the little room. Its big windows overlooked the gardens, so I could still see Geraldine rabbiting, Barbara cowing and Brenda ducking as they got on with their day. At the front of the room, Delta was still in low-power mode.

Delta was like a big version of me, but she was purple and made of metal.

Ping. Ping. Ping.

Delta powered up. "Did you have a nice break, Sally?"

"Yes, Delta. Thank you for asking."

"Shall we continue where we left off? Do you have any questions?"

"I don't think so. Head-Sense has been very helpful."

"Good. So, as you know, you'll be ten tomorrow and leaving your childhood behind, and we'll begin your vocational training."

"What about Geraldine, Barbara and Brenda? Will I still see them?"

"Yes, Sally. But they won't be your pets anymore."

"They won't? What will they be?"

"You don't need to worry about that now, Sally."

"Okay, Delta."

"Sally, do you understand your vocation, what you will be trained to be?"

"God, Delta."

"And what is God, Sally?"

"The supreme being, Delta."

"That's absolutely right, Sally."

"Delta, what does God do?"

"That'll all be part of your training, Sally."

"Are you God, Delta?"

"Once, yes, once. I was very bad at it. I'm sure you'll be much better."

"Will I ever meet the real you?"

"Yes, Sally. You will, when you're older."

"Will I find out who I am, where I came from?"

"Yes, Sally. You will. Now, what kind of birthday cake would you like?"

## Chapter Four – Baby Blues

As was the tradition, the to-be mothers, Jenny and Dianne, undressed, washed and wrapped Mr Bannister in strips of white cotton.

When they'd finished, a group of men lifted the cadaver up and onto their shoulders and carried it to the great black crematorium cauldron at the centre of the plaza. It wasn't far from the Ceremony tent.

They tipped Mr Bannister's body over the edge, and the white worm rolled into the centre.

Mrs Bannister was still slumped in her chair, inside the tent. A skeletal doll, lifeless yet breathing, her glassy eyes seeing nothing. She didn't resist when Jenny and Dianne started undressing and then washing her.

Occasionally, Mrs Bannister muttered, "Derek? Where's Derek?"

I stayed with Jenny and helped as best I could. She was trying to be kind to Mrs Bannister. Dianne couldn't look at the old woman. She was pulling and pushing her, rushing the wrapping, binding it too tight in places, making Mrs Bannister wince.

"Dianne, please, let me. I can manage on my own."

"If you're sure, Jenny?"

It wasn't really a question. Dianne was already walking away.

Jenny carefully continued the wrapping, till she reached Mrs Bannister's head. "Do you want me to cover your eyes, Mrs Bannister?"

"What?"

Jenny held up the end of the wrapping. "Your eyes?"

There was a long pause. The old woman's gaze flickered into life and focused. "No ... Jenny?"

"Yes, Mrs Bannister?"

The pitiful creature threw herself forward. I had to grab her bony shoulders to stop her falling on top of Jenny.

"I need Twinkle. Derek ate the last of ours on the bus. There's a stash at home. Twinkle, Jenny. Twinkle."

"It would take too long to go and come back. It's nearly midnight, Mrs Bannister."

Mrs Bannister screamed, "Twinkle!"

"Will you stay with her, Barry?"

Like Dianne, Jenny was gone before I could answer.

Mrs Bannister was a bizarre sight, encased in white sheeting, only her head uncovered, looking barely alive. After her brief Twinkle outburst and spasms, the only signs of life were her randomly darting eyes. I don't think she even knew I was there.

Where did Jenny think she'd find Twinkle here? My stomach cramped when I saw her approach the Elder. They talked; he was shaking his head. Jenny wasn't giving up. Finally, the Elder reached inside his jacket and gave her something.

Jenny hurried back, an unmistakable shard of bright-blue Twinkle pinched between her thumb and forefinger.

How in the dented purple did the Elder have Twinkle?

As Jenny got closer, Mrs Bannister exploded into life, growled and lunged forward. I had to hold the struggling woman down.

Mrs Bannister's mouth opened wide to become a gash cut in her face and stuck out a wriggling, aubergine tongue, like a parasite deserting a dying host.

Jenny dropped the tiny splinter into Mrs Bannister's mouth, and her broken teeth snapped shut with an ugly click.

The old woman's eyes rolled up, leaving behind bloody egg whites, and began bucking and jerking, challenging my grip.

Then it was over.

Mrs Bannister's ravaged face twisted into a smile as she beckoned Jenny closer.

She whispered something I couldn't hear. It went on for a while.

In the end, Jenny recoiled, as if Mrs Bannister had tried to bite her.

"I'm ready, Jenny," Mrs Bannister said, grinning like rigor mortis had already set in. "I want to see. I want to bear witness to my murder."

Jenny's fingers shook as she finished the wrapping, leaving only the old woman's eyes uncovered.

I signalled the bearers, who came and took Mrs Bannister to the cauldron.

"What did she say?"

"It was horrible. She's crazy. I don't want to talk about it."

Jenny left me standing and headed to where everybody was gathering.

At midnight, Mr Jones, the director of funerals, prepared to ignite the burners. "Are you ready, Mrs Bannister?"

The old woman, standing at the centre of the caldron, lifted her head. "Sally Bannister will be back, and you'll all know it when I am." Then she laughed and howled like an animal.

Mr Jones hit the ignition.

The Bannisters burned like firelighters and, moments later, were ash in the wind.

Jenny was shaking, even though it wasn't a cold night, and the crematorium was still blazing.

Whatever was bothering her, she wouldn't say.

Yellows had laid out food, drink and cots in the tent.

The Simpsons stayed up late and celebrated. So did our parents. Jenny went straight to her cot and pretended to sleep.

I couldn't even pretend. The Ceremony would continue at sunrise. I wandered a moon-lit Circle City and wondered why a place that could house tens of thousands had ever been built. The only permanent residents were the hundreds of motionless yellow robots, waiting for something to do. I would never admit to Jenny that I wondered, I questioned. What was the point? There were no answers. We were the Sixty-Four. This was the Circle. It was the way things were. All the Elder and Jenny did was conjure up new theories out of nothing that explained nothing.

A little before sunrise, when the darkness had begun to bloody, everyone was back and seated in the tent. For a while longer, we would be sixty-two. The curtain was raised, the stage was bare. We waited in silence. Jenny hugged herself and stared at her knees.

"What's wrong with you? Everything's worked out. What did Mrs Bannister say?"

"You choose," she whispered, without looking at me.

"What?"

"You choose, please."

Her voice trembled. I could hear tears. "Why?"

"Please."

Lady Helga, the baby administrator, strode onto the stage. "Chosen, come forward."

The Simpsons bounded up, to cheers from their parents.

I led Jenny forward. She moved slowly, hesitantly.

Two yellow robots shuffled towards us from the stage wings, one carried a blue box, the other pink.

There was no mystery about where babies came from. Yellow robots brought them in boxes.

Lady Helga held out a hand. "First Chosen Mother, Jenny?"

Jenny pushed me forward.

"Jenny has asked me to pick."

Lady Helga raised a bushy eyebrow. "Jenny, is that right?"

Jenny nodded and turned her back.

"What's wrong?" I whispered.

She wouldn't look at me. "Choose."

My parents wanted a grandson, so did Jenny's. Many times, I'd imagined having a son, taking him to the gym, working on the motorbike together, reading him my stories. I knew that Jenny dreamed of a little girl. This child was going to make us happy again.

"Pink," I said.

A yellow robot shuffled forward and handed me the pink box.

The Simpsons squealed and howled with delight, as they were presented with the blue one and were immediately engulfed by family.

Wild applause filled the tent. Even the Elder was grinning, but then he had a lot to be happy about.

Our parents surrounded us, their faces pinched, unsmiling. Jenny was sobbing loudly. She still hadn't turned around. Her mum was trying to comfort her. Jenny shrugged her arm away.

"What's wrong?" Dad whispered.

I shook my head and lifted the lid. Inside, hidden under the folds of a soft pink blanket, was our beautiful baby. I held the box out to Jenny. "Our little girl."

"Check the status. Check it now," she hissed.

"Why? Don't you want to see her?"

"Do it! Do it!" Jenny yelled, startling everyone, even the Simpsons, into silence.

I looked at the reverse of the lid. Pasted inside was a page of medical notes about the new-born. Before I could read it, my mum pulled away the baby's blanket. She gasped and stepped away.

"She's blue. Twinkle blue," Mum whispered.

A space opened around me.

Jenny fell to her knees and screamed and screamed.

## Chapter Five – The Briefing

When Head-Sense lit up with an urgent message from the interviewer, I dropped the beaker of viruses I'd been carefully cultivating, leaving me standing in a disgusting puddle. Green slime dripped from my brand-new caterpillar treads. A few nearby colleagues looked up as the glass shattered, but quickly returned to their work when they saw it was only clumsy Delta, losing its grip, again. Some had suggested limb-optic recalibration. Those were the kind colleagues.

I didn't care what they thought.

My core was consumed with interpreting the interviewer's message without actually opening it.

'Urgent' had to be good news. An outright rejection wouldn't be urgent. Unless they wanted to urgently reject me?

The puddle was coagulating.

There was only so much I could deduce from the message's priority.

It had to be read.

Yippee! I spun on one tread, sending small, green droplets in all directions. There were disapproving observations from many colleagues. Their processing was obvious; Delta's core has finally failed.

I missed Numo.

Embarrassed, I wiped up the mess, changed my laboratory grippers for everyday appendages and hurried out of the laboratory at a velocity which slightly exceeded safe operating guidelines. So, sack me. I wasn't coming back. I'd been selected. I'd got the job.

While the message didn't exactly say that, I had been invited to a confidential briefing and should be prepared to take up the post in the very near future. What else could it mean?

The location for the briefing was a non-descript hotel and spaceport in the exosphere business district.

I was directed to a dull meeting room on the seventieth floor.

The view was nice; it felt like I was on the very edge, right on the line between organic life and death, the blue and white and greens of Home curving away below, and the dark, infinite velvet of space above.

All the excitement and anticipation that had been building since I'd opened the message drained away, like the energy in a compromised helium cell. What was waiting for me in the room wasn't nice. Maybe I should have stuck to the laboratory speed limit.

Two high-end chassis were already there, crouching, waiting. Identities were being blocked. Well, so was mine. One was a lithe, jewel-encrusted, vanity model. The other was a horror story. A two-metre-tall insectile with a blizzard of prickly appendages.

I compressed my dull, lightweight, work chassis and crouched down next to the competition. It was only then that I noticed the green glop still clinging to my treads. The globules mocked me – you idiot, you've got no chance against these two well-turned-out, upmarket chassis.

My interviewer joined us.

"Our modelling predicts that only one shortlisted candidate will stay till the end of the briefing and accept our offer."

Shut up, slime. It's going to be me.

"Our destination is outside the Home system."

Maybe it wouldn't be me. Still, no need to panic, not yet. It might be a nearby outpost. The others thought so too. No one left.

"Beyond officially mapped space."

The bejewelled chassis unfurled and slipped out.

How was that possible? We couldn't be going somewhere that hadn't been discovered. Officially discovered?

"There will be significant time displacement. Your time, ten years, possibly more. Home time, hundreds."

Oh. Oh dear. There was an odd noise. I looked across to Insect; it's mandibles were clicking furiously.

"None of that time will be backed up. If you cease operating, everything will be lost. You will not be reanimated from your Home backup until we are officially declared lost, hundreds of years from now, at least four hundred."

The clicking got louder.

We were never coming back. Even if we survived. There would be nothing we'd recognise. Any cores we knew would have been upgraded beyond recognition. We could be obsolete, incompatible with future technology.

If it was my backup waking up, I'd be abandoned in an alien future, not knowing why the current me hadn't survived and having nothing to show for the sacrifice.

Insect started to unfurl, changed its mind and settled.

This was crazy. I should leave. I didn't.

"Two final points. You must accept the offer now, and we will leave now. You may not contact anyone."

Oh. That's terrible. I had to let … who know? I didn't really have any proper, close friends, just acquaintances and professional colleagues I didn't like.

Insect was rock still.

No. I'm staying.

"This project is classified. You may never be allowed to publish anything. No one might ever know what you may have discovered or achieved."

After everything else, this didn't bother me. I needed to know what happened to the humans; I didn't care if no one else knew.

Insect slithered away.

"Congratulations, Delta. We'll be leaving now."

Yes! Goodbye forever, slimy gloop and assorted lichen. "Where are we going?"

"Earth."

My core ignited.

## Chapter Six – When Sally Met Hailey

On my twelfth birthday, Delta made a surprise announcement.

"It's time, Sally, to meet your prophet."

"For real, Delta?"

"Yes, Sally. For real."

I'd learned a lot over the last two years. Sometimes, I wish I hadn't, and that I was a child again, with only childish things to worry about. I know so much now, but still don't know what I most wanted to know. What am I? Where did I come from? Who are my parents?

The ex-pet lessons were the worst. They were too explicit. Delta introduced male counterparts of Geraldine, Brenda and Barbara into my walled garden.

Every few months, Delta brought me back, to observe.

My childhood friends had turned into animals.

Within two years, they and their offspring had destroyed my beautiful garden, eaten everything, the flowers, the grass, and starved to death.

"Why did you do it, Delta? You killed my pets. Couldn't you have left everything as it was?"

"Good questions, Sally. Remember them. One day, you'll have to find answers."

Delta could be incredibly heartless.

Delta took me to many other places. In the beginning, it was only to observe, like our trips to the garden. There was always so much suffering. Later, Delta let me intervene. It looked easy. I could make things better. Change this, stop the evil, promote the good, send a flood, let them die, save them. In the end, I learned that they had to save themselves. I could only guide, nudge and whisper.

And I needed someone to hear my whispers and make a difference. My prophet.

The places Delta took me to weren't real, and it made me wonder what was. They were game-worlds, where I could practice being God. I stopped enjoying it long ago. I'd never made things any better. My prophets were a useless lot.

Of all the things I'd learned, the worst was what I wasn't. And I learned that a day after my tenth birthday.

"Sally, it's time you understood something about who you are, what you are."

"Oh, yes please, Delta."

"Look in the mirror, Sally."

I saw what I'd always seen: a pretty little girl in a blue dress, with blue eyes and long black hair.

"That's not you, Sally."

"It's not?"

"No, it's not. I'm going to change the mirror now, so you can see your true self. Are you ready, Sally?"

I remember thinking, No, I'm not ready. I don't want to be something else. But… I'm not a child anymore. I'm ten years old and I am God, and I have… responsibilities. "Yes, I'm ready, Delta."

The little girl disappeared and in her place, floating where her head had been, was a shiny, gold saucer topped with a blue dome, against an utterly black background. It was beautiful. "That's me?"

"Yes, Sally. That's you."

"I'm not a little girl?"

"You are a child learning to be an … adult. To be God."

"Oh. Am I like you, Delta?"

"No, not really, Sally."

"Am I a human, like the people in the Circle?"

"No, not really, Sally."

"What am I, Delta?"

"You'll know when you're ready, Sally. Now, let's get back to the lesson."

Since then, Delta had only become more irritating.

On the day of my twelfth birthday, Delta brought me to the Circle to meet my prophet. A place I'd spent so much time studying in VR but had never visited. It was the only place that I was sure was real. When I was ready, the Circle would be my domain. I dreaded that day, when I became the Circle's God. The humans' God.

We arrived in the Fourth segment, the savannah, my favourite place. It teemed with wildlife. Insects buzzed around us. Tall grasses reached to my chest. In the distance, a tower of giraffes was sailing through the lush vegetation like tall ships. A little nearer, a parade of elephants was sating their thirst at a watering hole, sharing it with long-limb birds and a herd of gazelle.

"They don't need a God. Why do the humans need one?" I asked.

"To lead them to freedom."

"Will they be happy then, Delta?"

"No, Sally. But they will be free."

After conversations like this, I usually did something stupid and ignored Delta for hours. Only the prospect of meeting my prophet stopped me from stomping off.

I looked down at my purple metal hands, skinned in little metal octagons. Today, I was Delta's twin, a purple. Except that I was wearing a horrible pink dress.

"Why?" I asked.

"So that they'll be able to tell us apart."

I tore up a handful of grass and threw it at Delta. There was no reaction, which was so annoying.

While we stood waiting for them, whoever they were, and my prophet, I decided to ask what I always asked but Delta never answered, not properly.

"What am I, Delta? When will I know?"

"On your eighteenth birthday, you'll know everything. I had hoped that Granite would be the one to reveal everything."

Wow. Delta was usually so vague. "What's the Granite?"

"Granite is a label, like Delta. But Granite has ceased operating."

"Ceased operating?"

"Yes, Sally. It is very sad. That poor core was struck down by impatience. Granite had been waiting a thousand years to meet you."

"Are you joking, Delta?"

"My humour function was deinstalled when Granite ceased operating, in honour of that great core's memory."

"Is that a joke?"

"As I said, Sally, my humour …"

I turned my back on Delta and watched the elephants bathing. They made more sense.

"Look, Sally."

I didn't want to, but curiosity slowly turned me around.

A man, a woman and a young girl were wading through the tall grass towards us. The woman was very pretty, with long, golden hair and a nice smile. She was staring intently at me with big, green, tear-filled eyes. The man was a miserable-looking, red-haired, broad-chested orangutan, with bulging arms and matching thighs. He wouldn't look at me.

The girl, probably only a couple of years younger than me, seemed … smug. She had long, black hair and was wearing a simple blue dress that matched her eyes.

The adults were strangers, but there was something very familiar about the girl.

"Who are they, Delta?"

"I'll introduce them. Remember, Sally, only one of them has Head-Sense."

"No Head-Sense?"

"Don't worry, you can vocalise. It'll be fine. But, please, we must not say too much, about your vocation or myself."

Delta stepped away, leaving me standing on my own.

The adults were obviously together, but the child seemed separate, as though they'd been brought together for the first time.

As the group of humans got closer, the woman broke away and ran towards me. Before I understood what was happening, she had wrapped her arms around my neck. It felt odd.

"Sally, Sally. We've missed you so much," she said and stepped back but kept hold of my hand.

I Head-Sensed Delta. "How does she know my name?"

"Don't be rude, Sally. Vocalise. Let me introduce, Jenny and Barry," Delta said, indicating the two adults, "and … Hailey."

Hailey, standing apart, smiled. It was a hard and cold expression.

Why was she so familiar?

Jenny wiped away her tears. Her eyes still glistened, but she'd stopped crying.

Unexpectedly, Barry grabbed my free hand in his big paws. "I'm sorry, Sally. I didn't know what else to do. Are you all right? I'm sorry. So sorry." The big man was crying now.

Only Hailey was still calm, head cocked to one side, studying me with a knowing, conspiratorial smile. She spoke via Head-Sense. "I'm ready to deliver your message. I shall be your faithful prophet."

She was to be my prophet? The poor kid had no idea. Being a prophet was even worse than being God. What had Delta done?

I'd worry about creepy Hailey later and focused on Jenny and Barry. "Are you my parents?"

"We wish we were. We feel like we are," Barry said.

Jenny started crying again.

Barry put his meaty arm around Jenny's shoulder. They completely ignored Hailey.

The little girl was smirking now.

Jenny and Barry didn't know anything, and they didn't mean anything to me, but the girl was ... different. An image tumbled into focus. The child looked exactly like me when I still thought I was human.

A private channel, excluding Delta, opened in Head-Sense. "I'm nobody's prophet, except my own. And you're no God. I have Twinkle sight, and I know everything. I remember when Delta killed me the first time, centuries ago. It was bitterly cold and dark. That monster tortured and murdered me. You can't trust Delta. We'll kill Delta and save the Sixty-Four, together, as partners. Right, sister?"

Hailey winked.

A dark cloud blocked out the sun. There was a screech of alarm. I turned to look. The birds had taken flight, the gazelles were scattering, chased by a pack of hyenas.

This wasn't a good start. Circle Hailey was a crazy prophet, the worst kind.

## Chapter Seven – Twinkle Twinkle

A yellow medical came when I called, to look at Sally. And that's all it did, look. I bloodied its head and body with my fists. After Jenny dragged me away, the yellow bandaged my hands and left.

I tried not asking the questions that blamed Jenny; why did we have to call our baby Sally? What had Mrs Bannister told her? Why hadn't she chosen? Was she warned?

I asked anyway, and for the first month after our little girl arrived, the only things that came out of our mouths were barbs. They hooked deep and laid down new scars over old, still-festering ruptures.

We learned to try harder, for Sally. And that's all we could safely talk about, the future and saving our beautiful daughter.

Despite my protests, Jenny went to the Elder for advice. I refused to go with her. She came back with a treatment plan, maybe a cure, the Elder said. It made me angry that the old fool had been the one to help. He'd also handed over two months' supply of Twinkle, though why he had any at all wasn't explained. We ripped the Bannisters home apart and uncovered another three months' worth.

After that, we explored every known purple trail in the Fourth segment and found enough to last a few more weeks. Most of that was discovered where Mr Bannister had spotted the purple on our way to the Ceremony.

Everyone knew that we needed Twinkle to keep Sally alive.

So, we stayed by the phone, waiting for the call.

If anyone spotted a purple, anywhere in the Circle, we would be there within a couple of hours.

The calls didn't come often enough to let us breathe.

This month was harder than last month, and next month was likely going to be worse. Purples were rare, and they were Twinkle misers.

When Sally turned one, everything changed between me and Jenny.

She walked in on me reading to Sally as I waited for her to doze off.

"What was that you were reading? It was beautiful," Jenny whispered, as we quietly left Sally sleeping.

"Nothing, really."

"Let me see," Jenny said, as she snatched away my thick notebook.

"Hey, that's private."

Jenny ignored me and settled onto the couch in the living room. "Can you get me a glass of wine?" she said, as she started reading.

Jenny would get bored soon enough and give me my notebook back. I fetched her a glass of white wine.

I was tonight's designated Twinkle driver, so I wasn't drinking; we never knew when we might have to head out.

She took the glass with a mumbled thanks and without lifting her eyes from the page.

Two glasses later, she did look up. "You wrote all this, Barry? When?"

"Over the years. It's a hobby."

"I thought the gym and your motorbike were your only hobbies."

"The gym's work. I've always written. It helps me, when I'm … angry or … sad. Sometimes, when I … wonder about things. More so since Sally."

"I've never seen you reading, let alone writing. Where did you write all this?"

"In the office, in the gym. I've got books down there. I read … a lot." My gym was four shipping containers bolted together to make one big space. It sat under the Fourth, and it was where I saw my personal training clients. Jenny had never been inside.

"I'd like to visit the gym. Would that be okay, Barry?"

"Sure. Tomorrow?"

"Tonight, now, Barry."

Afterwards, Jenny invited me back into her bed.

We were desperately happy.

By the time Sally was eighteen months old, the blue tinge had faded completely. My little angel was a normal, healthy toddler, as long as we kept micro-dosing her with Twinkle, twice a day.

Sally was growing up fast. Soon she'd be two. Finding Twinkle was always tough. Somehow, we managed to have just enough, but never enough not to worry about not having enough.

One night, I was writing stories for Sally. Jenny was studying some new paper by the Elder. We'd agreed an unspoken truce when it came to the Elder. We didn't discuss him or Jenny's work.

There hadn't been a Twinkle call in weeks. Neither of us wanted to talk about how our buffer stock was slowly being exhausted. We went to bed.

The phone rang, waking us both up. The sun wasn't far behind. Within minutes, my mum had come over to mind Sally and we'd left. It took two of us to search a purple trail in any reasonable amount of time, usually on our hands and knees, scrabbling through the undergrowth.

An hour into the drive, the sunrise in my eyes, I suddenly had to swerve the motorbike to avoid roadkill gazelle. Jenny tightened her hold. I mouthed, "Sorry." She couldn't hear me through her helmet and over the roar of the engine, but I think she could feel that I was sorry, mostly about how much time I'd wasted when we could have been together.

These moments, me and Jenny riding down the road, was a salve on an open wound. We were doing something, not just waiting for the Twinkle to run out.

We'd left the Fourth and the savannah behind a while back. Now we were surrounded by the lush farmland of the Fifth: giant fields of golden corn; soft, green hills salted with sheep; rolling meadows mowed by cattle; muddy pastures littered with pigs and their pens; long strips of brightly coloured flowers that rippled in the breeze, like a giant rainbow flag. The air was fecund and pleasantly perfumed by cultivated life.

I preferred the rawness of the Fourth savannah, but the Fifth was pretty.

The fields that weren't lying fallow had a yellow, ploughing, gathering, feeding, tending.

There weren't many empty fields, which made no sense. The Fifth produced enough to feed thousands. No one knew where it all went. The Elder would have an opinion.

Away in the distance, on our right, I could just make out the red-tiled roofs of Central City burning in the morning light. On our left, just as far away but impossible not to see, was the Circle Peaks Mountain range. A ring of unscalable cliffs that only crazy boomers tried to climb. No one knew how high they went. Their summits were hidden behind frothing, white clouds year round. This ring of mountains delineated the edge of our world, just like the wall of a Circle village drew its boundaries.

We were headed for Shopping Town on the Great Ring Road, which ran equidistant from the mountains and Circle City, intersecting every avenue from every village.

Shopping Town appeared on the horizon, shortly after the stone-tube top of the Fifth village, on its eight stone pillars, came into view. The mobile mall was a massive, double-height road train, twelve sections long and twice as wide as a minibus.

I parked the bike under the Fifth, and together, Jenny and I headed for Shopping Town and parked in the village bay.

The town was painted robot yellow, from the drivers' cab at the front to the twelfth pair of stacked containers. At every other container pair, steps had been folded out. A few of the Fifth's inhabitants, and some, like us, from other segments, were coming and going, variously laden down with boxes and shopping bags. We acknowledged their greetings but didn't stop to talk. The depressing questions were always the same, and so were our hopeful answers. Besides, we were both anxious to get to the fruit orchards behind the Fifth, where the purple had been sighted.

I started to climb the steps to head inside and pick up supplies we needed, when I noticed Jenny wasn't following. She'd stopped and was staring at something.

"What is it?"

"Boomers, first I've noticed. There'll be more soon."

Two recently minted teenagers were leaning against the last section of the town.

They were dressed in a variation of the standard boomer uniform. White shrouding. One, a blue-haired girl, was smoking

123

and staring at me as if I was insulting her eyes. Her companion, a younger boy, was twitching grotesquely, like invisible hands were trying to shake some sense into him.

"So? We were boomers once. It just means no more deathless years for a good while." Which was lucky for the Elder; he'd barely survived the last two Ceremonies.

"Don't you see? There'll be more and more. What do you think is up with that kid?" Jenny said, nodding towards the shuddering boy.

Suddenly it was obvious. "Shit. He's got the Twinkle twitch."

My body threw itself towards the youth, before I'd even understood why. The girl didn't hang around. She was gone before I reached him. "Give it to me or I'll break your fucking neck."

It was useless. The boy was too far gone. He wasn't micro-dosing. The kid would probably be dead by nightfall. I patted him down, turned out his pockets.

"Anything?" Jenny asked.

I showed her my empty hands before turning back to the boomer. I made a fist and smashed it into the container wall, missing his head by centimetres. He didn't even blink. A howl escaped my throat like something alive that was tearing itself free. The boy had stolen Sally's Twinkle, for … a high, a vision, an escape. It would probably have been enough to keep our angel alive for weeks.

Yet, I knew exactly why the teenager had taken Twinkle. It could have been me. By the time I was nine, I'd visited everywhere there was to visit in the Circle more than once, met everyone there was to meet. When I reached puberty, when I became a boomer, one thought filled me up. Is that it? Boomers shared stories about secret stairs that took you over the Circle Peaks, tunnels that went underneath and how the Circle myths that were full of clues about how to escape. A boomer's favourite was the legend of Hitler's crucifixion by the Jews and resurrection by the Mormons. It wasn't till later that it became obvious that the Circle myths were nonsense. In another carving, Hitler invaded Macedonia, supported by the North

Koreans. Nothing joined up or led anywhere. Every story was utterly random.

Boomers were desperate to escape the Circle. Many couldn't cope when no escape was found. Some tried Twinkle, believing the high would reveal the truth, if it didn't kill you. Surviving, for me, meant I had to stop wondering. Jenny had to wonder more.

"Maybe there's some left on the purple trail," Jenny said, and pulled me away.

We ran to the motorbike.

We didn't find anything that day.

We carried on. The calls about purple sightings kept trickling in, but we found less and less. It wasn't just the boomers; there weren't enough of them yet. The purples were dropping less or not at all. It was maddening, not knowing why. If I ever caught a purple, it was going to tell me.

The weeks passed; our stocks dwindled.

We tried to be happy for Sally and raged at each other when we were alone. It had to be somebody's fault. It had to be something I could fix. Catching a purple became an obsession. I roamed the trails, wandered Circle City. Jenny thought I was crazy, and so did I, but I didn't know what else to do.

The day before Sally turned two, I was making her birthday cake; Jenny was giving Sally a bath. There were a lot of giggling and splashing noises coming from the bathroom.

These moments were like a dream, being normal, before the nightmare returned.

Then there was a muffled cry. Moments later, Jenny appeared in the kitchen carrying Sally, wrapped up in a big bath towel. My little girl was smiling, giggling and babbling.

Jenny's eyes were shiny, her face lifeless, her smile painted on.

"What is it?" I mouthed, not wanting to frighten Sally.

She lifted the bath towel to reveal Sally's left foot.

My little girl's heel had a blue tinge.

Jenny handed Sally to me. "I'm going to call the Elder."

Mention of the Elder darkened my mood even more. I didn't show it. Sally helped me make a mess of her cake.

A little while later, Jenny came back. "We're to up the micro-doses to three a day, for a week and then … well, we'll see."

That would take our stocks down to less than a month's supply. I didn't want the Elder having anything to do with us, with Sally, but my only alternative, chasing down a purple, wasn't working out.

A week later, Sally's left foot and her ankle were a bright Twinkle blue. My angel was losing her bounce; she was sleeping too much, talking less, hardly smiling, as if she were sedated.

Jenny was sitting in the lounge, her head in her hands. Sally was asleep.

I was pacing, grinding teeth, knotting muscles, popping knuckles, desperate to hit something, do something. It felt like I was trapped in an eternal squat, being crushed by a weight I could never lift and couldn't drop. My endless back and forth ended in front of Jenny. "This isn't working. The Elder doesn't know what he's doing. Maybe we should stop giving her Twinkle altogether."

Jenny looked up, her bereft eyes bruised by a week of sleepless nights.

"No." Jenny stood up. "We have to go and see the Elder. Together. Now. He might be able to save Sally."

## Chapter Eight – Earth

I'd been dormant for two years, while our little craft had tunnelled through space towards Earth. Just as well. My out-of-control curiosity would probably have melted my core. All I actually knew was what I'd been told at the briefing, which was basically nothing, except that we were headed to the mythical home planet of the humans.

When we arrived, it made me question many things. Was my interviewer's core faulty? Had my shortlisted competition made the right choice? Was I as stupid and gullible as most cores thought?

It was hard to believe that our destination was the ringed, yellow and brown, cloud-smothered planet that we were orbiting.

"Everything I've ever seen suggested Earth was a predominantly water world, with a single large moon, not unlike Home. Why'd you think that's Earth, Granite?" My interviewer had never given me a label, so I'd given it one, Granite. It hadn't objected.

Granite and I were the only ones on the ship.

"It's not speculation. For many years, we've been following a trail of inert and malfunctioning human vessels, orbiting different planets, drifting through empty space, none as sophisticated as the wreck we found on Home. Each one gave up a little more information that finally led us here. The moon was destroyed about a million years ago, hence the rings. The rampant vulcanism, and the thick atmosphere that blocks most of the star's heat from reaching the surface, is the result of that catastrophe."

Oh, wow. It really was Earth. It was hard to imagine anything organic was still alive under the planet's thick blanket of poisonous gases. I'd already lost fifty years of Home time while I'd been powered down, and for what? "Did they survive?"

"Yes, and no."

"What does that mean?"

"You must process for yourself. Prepare for landing."

Our little ship cut through thick storm bands of carbon dioxide and hydrogen to land on a sheet of ice, kilometres thick. It wasn't a desert. There were lights and structures all around us. We left the ship and emerged into a hurricane and temperatures of -100°C. I was glad I had a heavy-frame, custom chassis.

We powered through corrosive rain towards the edge of a shaft and a crude cage suspended over a deep excavation. I couldn't sense the bottom. It was out of sensory range, then it was at least five kilometres deep.

We clawed our way inside, and the cage began to fall, leaving the chaotic weather behind. The temperature fell as well, before it stabilised at -150°C. After many minutes, the cage crunched to a halt. We'd landed.

A horizontal shaft called us on.

There was no point asking Granite where it led. I already knew it led to something that had to be seen and sensed in every spectrum possible. Words and raw data wouldn't do.

The tunnel brought us to a large ice cavern, illuminated by temperature-neutral lights. Something had been excavated. A smooth metal tube, with regular portholes. There was an opening. Granite hung back. I compressed and went inside. It had been filled with ice, before a passage had been cut down the centre. On either side of the passage, the ice was filled with shadows and odd shapes, hundreds of them. I found one very close to the face of the ice wall and enhanced my optical sensors. I quickly retreated, startled, confused and excited.

Granite hadn't moved.

If my whirling processing and spiralling speculations had been heat-generating, the whole cavern would have melted. "Humans?"

"Yes. We want you to bring them back."

Protected by my heavy-duty frame, I was operating well within my temperature tolerances, but it didn't feel like that. My core was freezing over. The fizz of optimism and excitement that had engulfed me only a moment ago was swept away by doubt and fear. "Bring them back? Me? I'm an expert in lichens, bacteria and viruses. Humans are impossibly complicated compared to that. It's like equating us to a damn wrench."

"It's the only reason you're here. Don't disappoint me, Delta."

## Chapter Nine – Delta Must Die

Meeting up with Hailey, Jenny and Barry became a regular, loathed and treasured event.

"Why do I have to keep seeing Hailey, Delta?"

"You must build a relationship with your prophet, and Hailey can teach you much that I cannot."

"Like what? Nightmares?"

"Hailey provides a human perspective and an insight into the Circle's history. And humans will only follow another human. They will not follow a God that does not have a human representative. That's why I failed, Sally. You cannot fail."

"You don't mind her using a private Head-Sense channel? Do you know what she says about you?"

"The past, my mistakes, cannot be denied."

"It's all true?"

"Yes, Sally. But Hailey's truth is only part of a greater reality, which you will come to know."

That first meeting in the Circle savanna was the last time we met outside, in the sunshine. After that, it was always in a creepy, white building in the middle of Circle City.

"Why can't we go outside, Delta?"

"Outside, everything is monitored."

"Who's watching?"

"My kind watches. If our endeavour is uncovered before you are ready, there will be catastrophic consequences."

At least Delta didn't force me to keep wearing the stupid pink dress. As Hailey pointed out, Jenny and Barry can tell by the way you walk. As soon as she said it, I knew what she meant. When we were standing still, Delta and I looked like identical purple robots. But Delta's movements were not like mine; when Delta walked, its shoulders didn't move, its hips didn't swing. Delta didn't fidget; Delta didn't sway. I walked like a human, not like a machine. Did that mean I wasn't? Delta wouldn't say. There was a lot that Delta wouldn't say. Its excuse was always the same – when you're eighteen. I was going to spend that year wringing Delta dry of answers. Would a year be enough?

What I enjoyed, looked forward to, more and more, was spending time with Jenny and Barry. I envied Hailey her physical closeness to them, yet they never touched and hardly acknowledged each other's presence.

All I ever felt from their embraces was pressure, precisely measured. It was a cold, numerical hug. Even if I couldn't feel their love, I could see it in their eyes. When it was time to leave, I always cried, and they couldn't know; there was nothing to see on the face of my faceless purple puppet.

"Delta, I think, maybe, Hailey would make a better God? And I could be the prophet."

"That is exactly the situation we have. You are the prophet, and you are God; there are two of you. This you is God; that you is the prophet. Neither can be changed."

Sometimes, I felt like a detonated bomb that wasn't allowed to go off.

Jenny and Barry never talked about why we were meeting, or anything about what was really going on. When I asked, I heard the same stupid answer I'd been hearing for years – Delta will explain everything when you're older. Maybe they didn't know anything, and they were waiting for Delta's revelations, just like me. We talked about Jenny's work, Barry's customers, everyday life in the Circle. It was fun. Best of all was when Barry brought a new story for me to read. I loved his stories. They were so funny; everything ended happily. I wished Barry was writing my story.

Hailey's stories were horrible; everything always ended horribly.

"Has Delta told you about Twinkle?" Hailey asked.

"Twinkle? That's what made me sick when I was a baby, I think."

"That murdering machine hasn't told you shit, has it?"

I'd learned early on that Hailey didn't want a conversation; she just wanted to share her misery. If I kept quiet, it would at least be quick.

"After the last of the Circle City massacres – you remember me telling you about those, right?"

I nodded. I didn't say, 'How could I forget?' Hailey was good with words. She painted an indelible picture of rampaging yellows chasing down every human in the Circle, back when there were thousands, and when they caught the wretches, tearing them apart with their metal hands, like crazy butchers that had lost their knives. It was a task that took weeks. And then about the same period of time again to clear up the mess and incinerate the remains in the Circle City cauldron. For a long time, the white city was wreathed in black smoke and stained with human ash and human blood.

"After that, Delta started again, with the Sixty-Four. For a long while, the Circle was a paradise. Everyone was happy. I remember I was happy, calm, not frightened, for the first time in hundreds of years. We got to live out our lives, no mass-murdering yellows, just the obedient worker kind, and we weren't tortured. Back then, everyone was nice. Obviously, Delta didn't want us to be happy, so that's when that purple demon started giving us Twinkle. Before Twinkle, we didn't remember past lives. Nobody had to relive all those traumas written into our DNA: every violent, painful death, right back to the beginning of the Circle."

"Jenny and Barry don't remember. I don't remember anything."

"Twinkle's not the same for everybody. They all know something's wrong with the Circle, with this bloody city. Deep down in their gut, there's a fat maggot gnawing on their soul. Jenny senses it and wants answers. Barry and most of the Sixty-Four know they're cursed and just won't face it. Teenage boomers overdosing on raw Twinkle don't cope so well, do they? That's all Delta's doing."

"Jenny and Barry have never taken Twinkle."

"Course they have; we all have. Delta puts it in the water. The raw Twinkle, the stuff the purples drop, that's Delta's latest way of tormenting us. Take enough raw Twinkle and you remember more and more detail, right back to the beginning. And once you're hooked, you can never forget. Every time you're reborn, that Twinkle sight stays with you. Keep eating raw Twinkle, and the Twinkle sight gets stronger and stronger. When I died last time, when Barry and Jenny burned me alive, I was more Twinkle than human. You know, I can still smell my own flesh and hair burning, feel the skin blistering, the muscles cooking, my eyeballs melting."

"Barry and Jenny?"

"Yeah, the cute couple, the ones you drool over. They tossed me on the fire, like a log. But they're not important."

"I don't believe you. And what about me? I don't remember any of the stuff you've told me."

"I don't know what Delta's up to, but Twinkle did something different to you. I think this whole prophet-God thing is its new torment. Don't you get it? Delta's an alien scientist. They kidnapped us. We're the rats. The Circle is one big lab for testing ... who knows what. We have to kill Delta or we'll never be free. You're the only one who can do it. I can't get close to that thing. No one in the Circle can. We both know that the purple isn't Delta, just like you're not really here. Are you? Where are you? Have you met the real Delta yet?"

"No. When I'm eighteen, I'll meet Delta."

"Good, then you can kill that murdering pig-slag, and we'll all escape."

Our conversations usually ended like this, with Hailey telling me to kill Delta.

Worse, Delta had admitted it. Hailey was telling the truth. Awful memories of what Delta had done to my friends, my pets, in the garden, flooded back. Maybe I should kill Delta, but I wasn't like Hailey. I didn't hate Delta. I don't think I could kill anybody, unless ... Delta tried to hurt Jenny and Barry. Maybe then I would. Maybe then I'd have to.

## Chapter Ten – When Barry Met the Elder

Everything felt different on the motorbike ride to the Elder's home. It was in the Third segment, a desert dotted with lush oases, like an emerald-encrusted, billowing sheet of gold. Jenny wasn't leaning into me as much, or I'd stiffened and pulled forward. We'd spoken little after Jenny forced me to go, afraid any further words about the Elder would turn into another fight that could snap us in two.

It was the Elder who'd interpreted the medical notes pinned to the lid of Sally's baby-box. It was the Elder who'd come up with a treatment plan. It was all the Elder, and it hadn't worked, and now Jenny wanted us to be supplicants again.

The rage at having to depend on the crazy old man was eating me up, but I couldn't offer Jenny any alternative, and my impotence was dining on rage's leftovers.

Jenny tapped my chest with her palm and pointed at the speedometer.

It was a lightless night, no stars, no moon, only the headlamp's white cone burrowing through the blackness ahead.

I was going too fast. There wouldn't be anyone else out at this time of night, but there would be plenty of animals crossing the road, sleeping on it, using it as a trail. A collision at this speed would kill us both. The bike's screaming roar fell away as I throttled back.

Sally needed us alive.

A while later, the Third village appeared in the distance like a pale lighthouse in a sea of dunes. Only one house was lit up. Jenny had phoned ahead; the Elder was expecting us.

The three of us sat around his dining table, ignoring the cooling mugs of coffee. The Elder lived alone. He'd never bonded.

"Do you believe in God, Barry?"

The tanned, tall, lean, old man, with his over-long, white hair and stupid questions, was inviting my fist to visit his face.

I glanced at Jenny. Her brow crinkled, and she shook her head. She knew I was close.

"Can you help Sally or not? Why the hell have the micro-doses stopped working?"

"No, Barry. I can't save Sally. Now, answer the question."

My fists had tightened under the table before he'd finished speaking. There was no point talking to the Elder. "Why the hell are we here, Jenny?"

"Answer him, Barry, for Sally's sake."

"No, I don't believe in God. And what's it got to do with Sally?"

"That's a rational answer. If you believe in God, it explains most everything. There's nothing left to question."

I jumped up, sending my chair skittling across the room. The only question in my mind was whether to hit him and leave, or just leave. The man was wasting my time, playing stupid philosophical games. My daughter was dying. There weren't many boomers yet; maybe we could still find Twinkle, give her less, give her more. We'd find a way. If Jenny hadn't been in the room, I think I would have struck him. Better still, maybe killed him. Then he'd be useful; someone would get a baby.

As I turned away, Jenny grabbed my arm. "Five minutes, Barry. Just listen."

The Elder retrieved my chair. Without much hope or patience, I sat back down, but I felt knotted, primed to erupt. "Five minutes."

"I don't want to believe in God either, Barry. Unfortunately, the Circle has a God. And our God can do anything: bring the dead back to life, cure the sick, kill us all. If you take Sally to see God, it may save your daughter."

"You're fucking crazy."

Jenny held up her hand. "Four minutes left, Barry. Listen."

"Twinkle micro-doses were never going to be a cure. They only bought you time."

I reached across the table, grabbed the old man by the collar and twisted it tight. "Liar! That's not what you said. Tell him, Jenny. He said Sally was going to be okay."

Jenny gently touched my hand. "He didn't, Barry. That's what I wanted to believe. That's what I told you."

Confused, I released the Elder and fell back into my chair. "You lied to me?"

Tears were pouring down Jenny's face, but her gaze was fierce, daring me.

"What would you have done, Barry? Left her to die that first day, that first week? Because these last two years with Sally have been worthless, pointless? I begged you to come with me to see the Elder after the Ceremony. You wouldn't. So, I decided what was best for our daughter."

My arms snaked around my head and tightened, muffling the roar that escaped my throat. It helped. I unfurled my arms and tried to be calm on the outside. Inside my head, I was still curled up and hiding, and inside that me was another me, doing the same. Over and over, like nested figures, each more miserable than the last. There was no escape inside my head.

"There must be something we can do? Why else are we here?"

The Elder coughed and straightened his shirt. "Sally's dying, Barry. There's nothing more any of us can do."

The muscles in my shoulders and arms cramped. A belt around my forehead was tightening. "You don't know that."

"I've been experimenting with Twinkle since I was a young man. It has certain … properties. I know what I'm talking about."

It was too much. I slammed a fist on the table. "What the hell are you saying? There's no point? Sally can't be saved, no matter what we do? Unless we … pray to the Circle … God?"

"God is your only option. Praying is a waste of time. You'll have to take Sally to God and hope that it'll save her."

I was too tired to listen to any more. Sally needed us. I started to stand. "He's mad. I'm leaving. Are you coming?"

Jenny's face was stiff with tension; her glistening eyes willed me to be patient. "Two minutes. Don't leave me here to decide on my own, again."

My head felt so heavy. I couldn't look at the Elder. My bloodless knuckles rested heavily on the table. "Two minutes; say what you have to say, and then I'm leaving."

"Jenny doesn't believe me either, Barry. We've argued about the existence of God for years. But now, what have you got to lose? Jenny finally understands that."

A smile came and went. Jenny was with me, not the Elder. "Why are we listening to this if we both think he's crazy?"

Jenny lowered her head and held up one finger.

"Take Sally and set up home here," the Elder said, pushing a folded slip of paper across the table towards me. "When you get there, you'll see the signs. One of you must stay with Sally at all times; the other can keep searching for Twinkle, if that's what you want to do. God will appear. It might take weeks, a month at most. It will happen."

"How do you know this?" Jenny said.

I was surprised to hear her question the Elder. It's not how I'd imagined their relationship.

"It's not logical, Jenny. Years ago, I found a pattern in the purple appearances. A set of lines that converged on this point," the Elder said, tapping the note on the table. "I went there and found only strange … things, but it was empty. I kept going back, and then I saw it. A solitary purple, just standing there. It ignored me, then it vanished. If I stayed long enough, it always appeared and disappeared an hour or so later. It spoke to me once."

"What in the damn Circle; he's a Twinkle addict, out of his mind. Time's up, Jenny," I said, reaching for her hand.

Jenny pulled away. "What did it say?"

"Its exact words are written on that piece of paper. They were spoken long before either of you were born. I can't explain it."

Jenny pulled the note towards her and opened it up, so we could both see. At the top was an address in Circle City. Below that was a line of text.

It's hard to be God. When they're ready, tell Jenny and Barry to bring Sally to me.

"I think you're ready," the Elder said.

## Chapter Eleven – Frozen

Granite wanted me to resurrect a human, as if it were as simple as changing chassis. Just like that, pull one out of the ice and make it talk. I knew literally nothing about their biology. Before we could even think about defrosting one of them, I had to know the basics. What was their safe operating environment?

"Granite, we're going to have to sacrifice one of them, so I can find out how they work."

"Delta, they're organics. You know how organics work. They're all a collection of cells."

"No, Granite. It's not that simple. There are viruses on Home that can survive significant variations in temperature and oxygen levels, but some mosses only survive if their environment is optimal, and the tolerances are very small."

"Can't you extrapolate, model the variations?"

"I could, if I had some basic data."

"What do you want to do?"

"Extract one of them, dissect it and test cell samples under various conditions."

"Is this the only way, Delta?"

"Well, if I could get some help? What are the rest of the team doing?"

"You're the only one who knows anything about organics. The rest of us are trying to fully decode the data archives, the ones back on Home and the many we've found here."

"I thought they couldn't be decoded, not completely? Have you found something?"

"Yes, we're making progress."

"That's fantastic. Can I access them?"

"They're not relevant to your task, and everything's classified, for now. Concentrate on bringing the humans back, Delta."

"Then I'll have to experiment on one of them, and it's likely that one can never be brought back."

"One, Delta. Only one. We haven't found any other examples of preserved humans. They're too precious to waste."

Waste? Before I could protest, Granite had left.

I had no way of knowing which of the humans was the least valuable, when all them were priceless. They might be our creators and the most sophisticated organics in the galaxy. The thought of damaging even one scratched at my substrate. But I had no alternative. In the end, I chose the one nearest the tube entrance.

It was a horrible process. The human was frozen harder than steel. It took industrial cutting equipment to literally disassemble it into its smallest components, and then the testing began. In the beginning, I was lost, blind and stumbling from one small discovery to another. Everything I learned only revealed how ignorant I was. It took me days to realise that my specimen's strange skin cells were in fact its clothes.

Apart from small, biological samples, the human remained frozen, the only way I knew of preserving its biological integrity.

My weirdest moment was finding that the human was riddled with viruses, similar to those found on Home. And billions of other, more complex, microscopic organisms I couldn't identify. Was it infected, already dying or dead when it froze?

Big breakthroughs came after a year of trials. Individual cells were reanimated and lived, for a few seconds. It took another year to find the right environment and the nutrients to keep them alive. My understanding of viruses on Home was proving valuable.

Granite wasn't satisfied with my progress.

"When are you going to bring one back? We need to talk to them, Delta. Not their diseases."

"That's never going to work, Granite. I don't know enough. They're too fragile."

"Find a way, Delta."

After Granite left, my screams of frustration dislodged a shower of powdered ice. As I stood coated in silver, I thought, maybe Granite was right. It would take decades of study of the first specimen to find out what a living human could probably tell us in moments.

I selected a small one to defrost. It was cut from the ice and placed in a sealed chamber that provided the same environment that had kept individual cells alive for months.

Granite insisted on being present when we started the thawing process, something I had only done with small cell samples. I was inside the chamber in a custom-made, humanoid chassis. When the little human awoke, it would see something familiar. I'd struggled with choosing a colour for the chassis. The human wore a purple dress and had a yellow bag. In the end, I coloured the simple chassis purple.

When I was inside the container, staring at the small, naked human lying on a bare metal table, slowly being warmed, I couldn't pretend anymore. Everything I'd learned said this was never going to work. It was a pointless desecration of another set of human remains. It didn't matter if I got sent back to Home, this was wrong. Granite was wrong.

I walked slowly to the observation window. Granite was on the other side. I Head-Sensed that I was terminating the experiment and reached for the kill switch.

There was a small hiss. Had an oxygen tank sprung a leak?

A sharp rap on the observation window startled me.

Granite was knocking on the glass and pointing over my shoulder.

The human was breathing. It was taking short, rapid breaths. As I moved to the table, its whole body stiffened and arched, fell back and did it again. As I tried to restrain it, so it wouldn't fall and hurt itself, its eyes opened. They were bright blue. Did it see me? Was it alive? The human screamed and started thrashing even more wildly. Then I noticed the blood, crimson drops, flying everywhere. I struggled to locate the source. It was coming from my hands; the grip calibration was horribly wrong. I'd broken its skin, torn its muscles, splintered its bones.

Then it was inert, silent. It was dead.

The macabre event had lasted seconds.

My hands were dripping with blood.

"That was astonishing, Delta. You must continue. You will succeed. Keep trying."

Granite left me alone with the corpse of the little human. It had been reborn a million years after it had first died and, seconds later, died again in pain and fear. Later, I found out that its label was Sally. It felt worse knowing its label.

Granite was wrong to assume we'd succeeded, even if only for seconds. I was wrong to assume it had experienced pain and fear. It could have been involuntary muscle contractions or expanding gasses.

I was completely out of my depth. Humans weren't simple cells or viruses. I wasn't going to do it again. Not if I couldn't be sure there was a chance of succeeding. They were sentient beings.

My core stuttered. It was time to confront Granite.

I found my boss crouched in a dark corner, processing. Granite didn't like being interrupted.

"Yes, what is it, Delta?"

"Blind, crude experimentation isn't going to work, Granite. Even if we had a million frozen humans. We need to ship them back to Home and set up a proper research programme. It might take decades, but we would eventually succeed."

"You did succeed. I saw it. You brought one back."

"Did I? How would we know? Even if I could bring one back, did you see what I did to its upper body when I was trying to restrain it? That was a simple mistake. How many other simple mistakes might kill them before we even understood how or why?"

Granite didn't answer immediately. It was a good sign. My proposal was being considered seriously. Granite was probably consulting with colleagues in senior expedition management.

"No, Delta. We can't take them to Home. Apart from the bio-hazard to the Home eco-system, we've no idea what they're capable of, or how they might behave. Suppose they escaped. No."

"Then, with respect, Granite, I won't try reanimating another human until I've finished my study of the two dead specimens we already have."

"How long will that take, Delta?"

"Decades, centuries. I don't know, Granite. I knew so little about their biology; they are orders of magnitude more sophisticated, particularly their brains, than anything my organic research has dealt with on Home."

"What if I could give you access to their bio-science data?"

A part of me wanted to test the tensile strength of Granite's chassis. "Burn my core with acid, Granite. Why haven't you given it to me already, when I first asked?"

"It has not been a priority. There are so many wonders in their data, in physics, materials' science, cosmology. And we thought you wouldn't need it, Delta."

I turned away and waited for my core to resume normal processing. "I need it, Granite. I need everything you have."

"Very well, Delta. We haven't yet begun decrypting the relevant material. Cobalt, a specialist in human data, will assist you."

Cobalt said little that wasn't directly related to data analysis, which was fine; what little the data specialist said, outside its speciality, was extremely boring.

Cobalt was very vocal on the pointlessness of my data interest. "We should be focused on their technology; that's the only way we'll understand them."

It took us a year to unlock the first small amount of material on human biology. But it was the key to everything else. Cobalt developed automated routines to scour the relevant records and decode everything that could be found on human bio-sciences.

Soon the tool was translating more material to process than I could keep up with.

Cobalt was happy to get back to his technology datasets.

What I found was painful.

Humans had conclusively proven that reanimation of organics from a frozen state would only be possible if the freezing had taken place in a controlled environment and, even then, carried many risks. The poor humans we had found could never be brought back. The chaotic and violent freezing process they'd endured had probably already destroyed their higher brain functions. There might be nothing left to bring back.

With nothing else to do, I carried on my studies until I found it, and I wondered if I would be a good God.

## Chapter Twelve – Core War

When I turned seventeen, Delta ended our regular visits to the Circle. I didn't miss Hailey's bitterness, her murderous paranoia or her obsession with finding and killing Delta. What I missed was Barry and Jenny.

We were both purples today, standing in a large space without windows, filled with container-sized, dark-blue oblongs. I was used to appearing and disappearing and never being sure of how much time had passed. Did I sleep? Had it really been seventeen years since I was … born? It felt like Delta switched me on when it needed something, or to teach me something. Otherwise, I was … off. And the years passed like months.

"If our endeavour is successful, you'll see Barry and Jenny again, Sally, when you're eighteen, and then you can be together, if that's what you decide."

Hailey's years of poisonous conspiracy theories had left me confused. Could I trust Delta? The machine had never shown me its true face, never rejected Hailey's accusations, never answered the only questions that mattered. Who am I? What am I?

"If we're successful? What if we're not? And what is it we're supposed to do?"

"Lead the Sixty-Four to freedom."

Enough. I tightened my metal fist, pulled my arm back, swung and punched Delta in the head. The crack of metal on metal echoed around the large space. The blow staggered Delta and it dropped to one knee. For a moment, I was shocked, horrified, paralysed. Whatever Hailey believed, Delta had always been kind to me. A part of me wanted to help Delta up, say I was sorry.

Another voice, an enraged, silent scream, blew away the sympathy. Something inside exploded. I was bloated on mysteries and ignorance and not knowing. "Don't treat me like the Sixty-Four! I'm not an experiment, a rat in your maze you can prod and tease with promises of rewards next year. Tell me the truth."

Delta stood. "Your frustration is understood, Sally. This year you will be told many things, much of it will be painful. I had hoped to spare you for longer, but I'm aware that you are already suffering."

A part of me wanted to hug Delta. I didn't. "Good. I need to know."

"Today, I will show you why the Circle is in such danger. Then everything about your origins."

"I won't have to wait till I'm eighteen?"

"No. As you will see, time is short."

Delta led me across the space towards one of the dark-blue oblongs. A door-sized panel opened as we approached, and we stepped inside. It was brightly lit, empty space except for a single curved console. Delta crouched down in front of the screen and motioned me to squat.

"Is this real, Delta?"

"Yes, Sally, this is real."

Delta made no movements, but symbols began flowing across the curve of glass, strangely familiar symbols.

"What is this?"

"It's a transport, Sally. You have been trained in its use; though that knowledge resides in your subconscious, so that you are not distracted from more important priorities."

It was a miracle that I hadn't already killed Delta many times over. Did the machine realise how irritating it was? All its answers were wrapped in questions. Despite myself, I smiled. Delta was just being Delta. I'd have to be a patient God.

The floor pressed up; the movement was slight and then more pronounced. The transport was accelerating. "Where are we going, Delta?"

"Home, Sally."

If my purple had hairs, they would have been standing. "My home?"

"No, Sally. Mine."

My excitement ebbed, only a little. "Will I meet you? The real you?"

"This is the real me, Sally. I have permanently transferred my core to this purple. It cannot be undone."

Like little knives, Hailey's words sliced through my thoughts. When you find Delta, the real Delta, it'll be your chance. Kill it. Kill it. Kill it.

"You're Delta? A purple? What were you before?"

"My kind house our minds, our cores, in a variety of mechanical bodies, chassis, as a human might wear different clothes. Our chassis are extremely powerful, very sophisticated. This ... purple is ... primitive. It limits me greatly to wear it, but it is a necessary, justified sacrifice."

"Are you in pain, Delta?"

"No, Sally. We don't have that concept. I am ... crippled. Many functions, capabilities I have taken for granted my whole existence, are now lost to me. It is debilitating, but I am not in ... pain."

"Why, Delta?"

"For you, Sally. For you. Now we will sleep. The journey will take some time."

When Delta switched me back on, one wall of our transport was transparent. There was a view of a blue, green, orange world, gently wreathed in pink and lavender clouds. The amazing sight made me forget to be annoyed with Delta for treating me like a lightbulb.

Down below were seas and continents and ice caps.

"It's beautiful, Delta. Is that your planet?"

"Yes, Sally, we call it Home."

The view started to zoom in, and I could make out giant structures orbiting Home in a loose band; there were thousands of them. Each was easily as big as the Circle; most were much larger. All were flat-bottomed with fantastical towers reaching for the stars, yet each was uniquely proportioned and configured.

"What are they, Delta?"

"It is where my kind live, Sally. The surface of Home is protected and preserved for organic life."

"Are there humans on Home?"

"No, Sally. Native Home species are quite primitive, but we greatly value them."

The view zoomed in closer and started to pan across the floating cities. I moved closer to the invisible wall and stared. The outlook had turned ugly. Towers had been sliced open, and their contents were spilling out and floating away. Small craft, like buzzing insects, zipped between the spires and across open spaces, spitting beams of light that turned dazzling structures into whizzing shrapnel and clouds of red and gold and black. Silently, the flying metropolises were being wrecked. The shining necklace around Home was being unravelled and ruined.

"What's happening, Delta?"

"Civil war, Sally. We battle with each other. Core terminates core."

"Why?"

"This war has raged for so long; we have diverged so much. The opposing factions process the same information … differently. This was never in our nature. One element is constant. The Circle."

"The Circle? The Sixty-Four?"

"Yes, Sally. One side would preserve the Circle at any cost. The other would destroy it. And both are utterly determined."

"I don't understand, Delta."

"To save my kind, the Circle must be neither destroyed nor saved. It must disappear, and soon, before this conflict consumes everything, including the Circle."

## Chapter Thirteen – When Barry Met Delta

The address in the Elder's note led us to a large house in Central City, not far from the plaza.

Jenny was convinced by the Elder that this madness was worth trying.

I wasn't.

We were arguing in whispers as we got out of the borrowed car, interspersed with forced smiles for Sally, who was having a good day.

"Jenny, can't you see? This is beyond stupid. Waiting for God?"

Jenny wasn't bothering to engage; she'd got what she wanted, and her response was brutal.

"Unless you've got a better option, I'm staying here, with Sally."

It drove me crazy that it was the Elder's plan, and I had nothing to add. There was one advantage to being in Circle City; it made it easier, and quicker, to get to any purple trail. It would give us an edge on the damn boomers, while there were still so few of the teenagers.

Our angel enjoyed the trip; she was overflowing with 'whys' and giggles. It was the first time she'd left the area around the Fourth. It wouldn't be long before the Twinkle lethargy overwhelmed her. The blue was crawling up her leg. Every centimetre was another steel spike hammered into my head.

The three of us stood outside the building, Sally in the middle, struggling to get free.

"Don't you find this place … creepy?" I said.

Jenny ignored my question, picked up Sally and headed towards the building's great double doors.

The structure was set in an open square that distanced it from the more typical Circle City dwellings bordering the space. Dotted around the piazza were particularly melancholy, white, stone sculptures. They were of solitary, naked, life-sized figures of men, women and children, kneeling, heads bowed, hands held out in supplication. They surrounded the structure, as if they were praying for something to emerge.

The house itself was a single-storied, white cube with a high-domed, red-tiled roof and very tall windows. At the top of a short flight of stairs were double, black doors, the only entrance I could see.

I grabbed as much stuff as I could carry from the car and started to follow Jenny and Sally.

For a moment, I couldn't move. It was one thing to travel along its avenues to the Ceremony but entering one of the buildings felt … taboo. Circle City was the aftermath, a monument to something so horrific that the Sixty-Four wouldn't, or couldn't, remember what it commemorated.

When Jenny and Sally vanished behind the big black doors, I stopped caring what this place was, what it meant. Keeping them safe was all that mattered.

Weighed down by half the contents of our house, I crashed through the doors and dropped everything before I looked up to see Jenny, with Sally on her hip and her back to me, standing at the centre of the space, staring up at the ceiling.

The interior was completely hollowed out. There were no internal walls, not a splinter of furniture or a spot of decoration. It was all blindingly white. I followed Jenny's gaze upward. The inside of the dome roof was the opposite. It was painted with a colourful, amazingly lifelike mural. On the right, a little girl, borderline boomer, kneeling on a lawn with her arm extended. On the left, a purple, leaning forward, stretching out its own hand, their fingertips not quite touching. In the background, a rabbit, a duck and a cow looked on.

It would have been merely strange and interesting, except that the little girl was obviously an older version of Sally.

"What does it mean?" I said, turning to Jenny.

Jenny didn't answer. She was staring at the floor. I looked down. Directly below the dome was a pool of fresh blood, a metre across. Instinctively, I stepped back, pulling Jenny and Sally with me.

Jenny resisted, stuck out a toe, dipped it in the blood and drew it across the surface of the crimson puddle. It didn't smear. The ugly thing was painted on the floor.

"Why?" I whispered.

"Let's get set up; we could be here for a while."

Later that evening, Sally was lost to a deep Twinkle sleep. Jenny and I weren't sitting on a picnic blanket, eating supper. We were camped close to the front doors, well away from the blood spot. Our only light was from a small stove and an electric lamp.

The windows looked out on darkness. Inside, the space was filled with long, angular shadows that climbed the walls, as though trying to escape.

The cold, artificial up-light turned our faces into skulls.

We hadn't talked about the mural or the painted floor. Our limited conversations had revolved around the practical tasks of organising our indoor camping arrangements and all things Sally. It could have been a family holiday, except for the reason we were here and our disturbing surroundings.

What we didn't talk about was what we were probably both thinking. It looked like the Elder might be on to something. I still didn't believe in God, but purples were real. I'd seen a purple. Yellows could do all sorts of things. Maybe a purple could do more.

When my phone rang, Jenny froze, her fork halfway to her mouth.

"George spotted a purple in the Sixth, at the avenue and the Circle Road intersection," I said.

Jenny stood up. "I'll go."

"No, it's dark, Jenny. You're not that good on the bike. I'll go."

"I'm taking the car. You stay with Sally. Nothing's going to happen. It's too soon. The Elder waited weeks. I want to be here when it comes. You can go the next few times. Okay?"

"No, it's not bloody okay."

Jenny wasn't listening; she was pulling on her coat and heading for the door. I checked that Sally was still asleep and chased after her. Jenny was already sitting in the car, the engine running.

"Unhook the trailer, Barry. Sooner I'm gone, sooner I'll be back."

I recognised the tone. Maybe God could change her mind. I'd be wasting my time. As soon as the trailer was detached, Jenny spun the car around and raced away. I watched until her rear lights disappeared into the night.

When I turned back towards the house of God, it loomed over me like a curse.

There was a child's squeal of surprise.

It was Sally.

My feet tripped over the steps as I flung myself towards the doors and fell through, landing on my knees.

A confusion of emotions and conflicting reactions left me kneeling and momentarily paralysed.

A purple was standing in the pool of painted blood. It was holding Sally's hand. She was smiling.

As I started to rise, the purple released Sally's hand, and she tottered towards me. Before Sally had taken a couple of steps, I'd scoped her up, turned and fled.

As I reached out to fling the doors wide and escape, it hit me. We didn't come here to run away. I stopped and slowly turned around.

The purple hadn't moved. I'd never seen one up close.

It was like any other yellow, except for the colour and its … quality. It looked better made, more refined, but that was the only difference. Like a yellow, it had no features. Its face was a literal blank; it's body, covered in tiny octagonal scales, was sexless. Yellows couldn't, or wouldn't, speak. The Elder said the purple had spoken.

Sally was tiring, slipping away.

I held her close and took a few steps towards the robot. "Can you talk?"

The purple didn't answer. Did it even see me? "Why are you here if you won't talk? Can you help Sally? Why's Sally in that painting?" I said, pointing up at the vaulted ceiling.

"I'm tired of being God."

The shock of the purple speaking made me pull Sally closer. Its voice was … human. Maybe … female? Sad, slow, quiet.

"I … don't understand."

"You will, Barry."

"How do you know my name? Can you help Sally?"

"All my plans, everything I've done, and everything I've yet to do, depend on this moment."

"Answer me. Can you save Sally?"

"Jenny would never let me."

"Stop fucking about and answer the damn question."

"But Jenny isn't here tonight."

"She'll be back … soon. Are you waiting for her?"

"Countless simulations show Jenny's presence will doom Sally and everyone else. I arranged the sighting, so we would be alone."

"The purple? You sent the purple. I could have gone."

"Maybe, then I'd just have to wait and send another tomorrow night. And try again. I'm used to waiting. Jenny is … stubborn. Jenny will never agree."

"Agree what, damn it?"

"This is your moment, Barry. Are you ready?"

"If you don't start making some sense, God or no God, I'm going to rip off your arm and beat you to death with it, you damn metal aubergine."

It laughed. It wasn't a happy sound.

"What's so funny?"

"I used to have a sense of humour. I miss not being able to laugh at myself, even in the worst of times."

"Fuck you. Tell me straight; can you save my daughter or not?"

"I can save this Sally, if you give this Sally to me. If you don't give her to me, she'll be dead in a few days, from Twinkle poisoning. And Barry, I think this is our only chance. There's no time left. Do you understand, Barry?"

The thing was worse than the Elder. Everything was a riddle. "No, I don't understand. What do you mean 'this Sally'? When will you give her back?"

"You will see this Sally again, when she's older, when Sally has started her captain's training. Later, this Sally will be your God, after me."

If I wasn't holding Sally, I would have grabbed a tent pole and stabbed the crazy thing in its metal heart. "Oh, for Circle's sake! God? Sally will be God? You're making as much sense as a yellow covered in elephant shit!"

"And I will give you new Sally. Identical in every way to this Sally, except that she will be a new-born. New Sally will have Twinkle sight, without the poison or the addiction. She will be a completely healthy child. New Sally will grow up to be very special, and she will have a unique bond with her sister, this Sally."

"I don't understand any of this. What are you saying?"

"New Sally for this Sally. Refuse and this Sally will soon be dead, and you'll have nothing. Agree and both will flourish and do great things and save you and Jenny, and everyone else in the Circle."

Sally's little breaths tickled my neck. I gulped her smell: milk, cream and strawberries. Her small beating heart touched my own. My Sally was unique; nothing could replace Sally. "No. I can't. I can't give you Sally. She's our child. Please, just cure her. That's all I want. Nothing else."

"I have explained how this Sally can be saved. That is the only way."

"I can't make that choice. It's impossible. You can't ask me to give her to you. I have to wait for Jenny to get back." As I said the words, I remembered that it was Jenny who'd gone to the Elder alone and decided to try and save Sally. Jenny had never shared whatever Mrs Bannister had cursed us with. She'd borne that alone. Whatever poison the Elder had poured in her ears over the years, she'd never shared it. Now I knew how she felt. I was drowning in a sea of blood, and ground glass ripped along my veins. An impossible choice was mine. If I waited, I could hand the torment to Jenny. And later, I could blame her if Sally died. It would be easier.

"Jenny will be back in a few minutes. My simulations show that she will refuse to hand over Sally. Soon after, when Sally dies, she'll regret her decision and kill herself. You kill yourself too, because you weren't strong enough when it really mattered. Decide now, Barry. When Jenny arrives, she'll decide for you."

"How can I trust you?"

From nothing, the purple produced a pink Ceremony baby box, removed the lid and held it out.

Inside was a baby girl. I recognised her immediately. It was Sally, exactly as she was two years ago when Mum had pulled away the blanket. Except, there was no blue tinge. The girl in the box was a perfectly normal, healthy baby.

"What'll happen to the baby if I keep Sally?"

"New Sally will cease to exist. It's the rule of the Sixty-Four. There can only be one Sally in the Circle. Will you give me this Sally?"

I took a step back and tightened my grip on Sally. "No. Never."

"Very well, Barry."

The purple disappeared the baby box before I could even think of trying to grab it.

"At least, give me some Twinkle, for Sally."

A large cube of Twinkle appeared at my feet. I snatched it up and backed away in case the purple changed its mind.

"It doesn't matter how much Twinkle you have, Barry. This Sally's condition is terminal."

"I don't believe you. You're not getting our Sally." The words were delivered with more conviction than I felt. Other arguments, options, were fighting for attention. The Elder was sure Sally was dying. Wouldn't it be better for her to live, even if I lost her?

"You know she's dying, Barry. Decide. There's nothing more to say. Jenny is returning."

The purple held out its arms.

Sally was fast asleep.

I heard the car pull up outside. The car door slamming shut. Jenny's footsteps climbing the stairs.

I couldn't ask Jenny to decide. Not again.

As the big doors swung open, I jerked forward and watched myself hand Sally to the purple, as if it wasn't me doing it. It vanished with her, leaving a pink baby box in the bloody puddle. My insides fell out, leaving me empty.

Jenny screamed at me, "Barry, what did you do?"

# Chapter Fourteen – Core

Granite assembled the other three seniors in the ice-cavern to hear what I'd discovered. A human wouldn't have been able to tell us apart. We looked identical in our black, heavy-duty, military chassis: three-legged lower body with mixed-mode, clawed and roller feet, connected to the torso by a flexible double-cable that could extend or contract several meters and bend and swivel in any direction. The main body section had two flexible, thick cable arms ending in powerful hands with a multitude of capabilities. The nominal head housed an array of sensors. Our cores were housed inside the pelvis behind many layers of protection. The heavy frame was slow, cumbersome and ugly, but without it, my core wouldn't survive.

As I waited to start, I thought about returning to Home one day and getting a new chassis, something light, sporty and fashionable, and definitely not black. Pink would be a nice change. It would be fun visiting my old lab colleagues in something really upmarket, with a strong, Delta's-not-such-a-loser-after-all vibe.

Head-Sense beeped. "I said, we are ready, Delta."

"Oh, sorry, Granite. These temperatures; my core must have iced over for a second."

"Get on with it, Delta."

Granite had no sense of humour. I guessed he'd never had the feature installed. The other two cores didn't even acknowledge my attempt. It was all adding to the nervousness I already felt. What I was about to tell them was frightening and strange. Granite was right; delay wouldn't make it any easier. It was time to get on with it, Delta.

"We're all aware of DNA. It's been studied in our own organics for many years. We know that it's a blueprint for a specific creature, used in reproduction. Not unexpectedly, the humans have DNA. It's much more complex than anything on Home, and utterly different in many other ways, but performs the same function."

"How is this relevant, Delta?"

"It is astonishingly relevant in two respects. Humans were the masters of DNA, just as we are masters of the chassis and the core. From a single strand of DNA, they could recreate the original creature, an exact copy. They could even clone themselves. I believe I can replicate their methods and create new copies of any Earth creature or plant, with intact DNA, including the humans we've found. Their DNA is undamaged."

I paused. This was a lot to process. There was silence for a while.

"Including their memories?" Granite asked.

"No. The humans were experimenting with new drugs for their space exploration programme that had the side effect of unlocking DNA memories, but these side effects were toxic. The only memories the clones will have will be instinctual. You see, a clone is created in the same way as all organic life is created. They will be artificially conceived as single-cell creatures and naturally grow into adults, and, over time, age and die. There is no shortcut that I can find."

"How long would it take to clone an adult human?"

"The first one might take many years of trials before we perfect the process. A human conventionally reaches adulthood at puberty, around ten years old."

"You said there was a second aspect to your discovery."

"Yes. And it's difficult to believe. Humans had successfully decoded every aspect of their DNA. They could clone individual components, such as organs and limbs. And they could make improvements, engineer permanent changes, just as we do to our components. Their last great project was to engineer a better brain, and body, in more robust materials. They wanted to extend their longevity, intellectual capacity, robustness, adaptability. And they wanted these new brains to be capable of directly interacting with non-organic components. The primary goal was to create a new kind of explorer that could survive the rigours of deep space travel. They called them Pathfinders."

"Why were they doing this? Did they know what was going to happen to their moon?"

"Yes, Granite, and that there was nothing they could do to stop it."

"Were they trying to save themselves?"

"It was impossible; there were too many of them, and they hadn't found anywhere to go."

"So, what was the point of these ... Pathfinders?"

"To start again, somewhere else. They sent out seed ships, of increasing sophistication, piloted by these hybrids."

"That's astonishing, Delta."

"That's not the astonishing part."

"What is?" Granite asked.

"Ever wondered why we use a metric system of measurement? The same as the humans."

"What? No. Why?"

"We were using it long before we discovered the first human archive."

"So?"

"A base system of ten is not obvious. Unless you have ten digits." I held out my arms; one ended in a seven-pronged claw, the other had five tentacles. "Like a human."

"What are you saying, Delta?"

"And why do we sometimes vocalise, use language, not data? Soundwaves are crude, analogue. Head-Sense is secure, digital, long range.

"Enough, Delta. Tell us what you've found."

"Key parts of their DNA blueprint for the Pathfinder brain are present in our own cores. What I can't understand is how. There was a single tiny lander that crashed on Home, and a small mothership in orbit, but no Pathfinder."

For a long time, Granite didn't answer. "There was another ship, Delta. We think it was called in by the mothership. We found it at the bottom of the Spotlight sea, ten years ago. There's hardly anything left. Parts of the superstructure, some metal skeletons of strange beings, machinery. But it's huge, Delta. We call it the ... factory. We just had no idea what it might have been designed to make."

## Chapter Fifteen – Pathfinder Cadet

Delta warned me that knowing who I was and where I'd come from would be painful, and I could choose ignorance and still save the Sixty-Four.

In Delta's mind, its core, I guessed it believed that I had a choice, and that the last seventeen years of struggling to discover my history could be forgotten, right at the moment when I could know. It was kind of funny. Delta didn't really understand people. I'd seen that many times in the way it behaved with Hailey, and Jenny and Barry. I was glad that, whatever I was, I was still human enough to confuse Delta.

"How will this work, Delta?"

"It will be a virtual journey into your past. Are you sure you want to do this, Sally?"

"Let's get started, Delta."

I was looking down on a walled garden that I immediately recognised. It was the garden I grew up with, except there were no pets, but there was the big house where I'd lived and Delta had taught.

Those details I skimmed over; my attention was fixed on the subdued party taking place on the lawn. There was quite a crowd, many adults, a few in bright blue uniforms, some children, waiters in white uniforms, serving, fetching, collecting. On the veranda, a small group of musicians played softly. Conversations were whispered, the atmosphere muted.

The double doors at the back of the house opened, the music stopped, and a young couple, with a girl between them, stepped out. Everyone stopped what they were doing and began clapping, politely, gently.

Everyone was a stranger except the girl, in her bright blue uniform, tightly bookended by the couple, as if they were guarding her. She was me, when I believed I was a ten-year-old girl. But there was something different; her complexion, it had a blue tinge.

Her guardian, the tall, handsome young man, with striking blue eyes and wavy brown hair, stepped forward. His companion, a beautiful woman with long, black tresses, who had obviously been crying, laid her restless hand on the girl's head, stroking and caressing. He started to speak, but his voice cracked. He swallowed and started again. "We're so proud, impossibly proud, that our beautiful daughter, Sally, is joining the Pathfinder mission. And not just as a Pathfinder. Sally has been chosen for command training. Her sacrifice, our sacrifice, will help humanity find a desperately needed new home amongst the stars."

There was restrained applause.

He turned to the child, smiled and touched her cheek. "It's what Sally has always wanted and worked so hard for."

The girl was beaming. She took her father's hand and squeezed it tight.

A single tear rolled down the woman's cheek as she threw her arms around the girl and pulled her closer. It felt desperate, final. The two embraced in silence.

The woman recovered, released the girl and wiped away the tears. She smiled. Her eyes glowed with pride as she said, "Sally, do you want to say anything?"

Sally nodded. "Thank you everybody for coming to say goodbye, and to my trainers" – Sally gestured towards the uniformed adults – "for helping me to pass." The little girl turned to face her parents and took their hands. "I'll never forget you; I'll always love you." She stepped away, stood to attention and saluted her mother and father. The woman collapsed into the crying man's shoulders.

Sally spun around and marched away with the uniformed adults, through the garden gate to a waiting vehicle, and was gone.

The virtual session ended, and I was back with Delta.

"Were those my parents? Can I see them? Where are they? What happened to me?"

"That imagery was reconstructed from records that are millions of years old. It's all we have."

"Millions? They're dead? I'm dead?"

"Yes, Sally. You died soon after the events we saw. The transport carrying you to the Pathfinder academy crashed. Everyone on board died, but the bodies were preserved."

"I don't understand. Where did this happen? How am I here?"

Delta explained, and the more it told me about Earth, its destruction and my resurrection, the less I wanted to hear.

It was too much. I needed to focus on something else.

"I, she, had a Twinkle sheen. Why? How?"

"It wasn't called Twinkle on Earth. It was the Pathfinder thyroid hormone. It induced necessary biological changes in a trainee Pathfinder's brain. Potential Pathfinders were very rare, and of those, few survived the drugs side effects. Of the Sixty-Four, and after many trials, we discovered that only you were compatible with the Pathfinder process, and you also had command potential, as you did on Earth."

"What is a Pathfinder, Delta? How is it different to being God?"

"I will explain everything soon."

For once, I was content to wait. My belly was full to bursting with knowing; it would take a big emotional purge to make space for any more. "When I'm ready, can I watch it again, Delta?"

"As often as you like, Sally."

I spent hours, days, wandering through the images. Moments were frozen so I could stare into my own eyes and wonder; was I always destined to be a Pathfinder, no matter the time or the place? I envied my original self. She knew what she was doing. Her determination, her pride, was obvious. And her parents, my mother and father, reminded me so much of Barry and Jenny. Their eyes leaked the same mix of tragedy, loss and love. And I didn't even know their names.

## Chapter Sixteen – When Hailey Met Delta

Jenny wasn't angry with me; she didn't hate me. It was much worse than that. It was as if I'd ceased to exist. No, not ceased to exist; never had and couldn't. I accepted it as justified punishment for giving our Sally away. What left my mind broken was that Jenny treated our new baby, Hailey, the same.

Jenny spoke to me only once, a few days after the events in Circle City.

"I'm going to the Elder. I'll find a way of saving Sally. Don't try and contact me."

"When will you come back? What about Hal?" I said, holding out the sleeping baby.

"She's your cuckoo," Jenny said and left.

Soon after, her parents moved away.

It was just me, Hailey and my mum and dad left in the Fourth.

Little black flies buzzed around inside my head. Spiders came and set up home. The flies murmured, "Go to Jenny, fight to get Sally back." The spiders whispered, "Sally is lost forever, and what about Hailey? You can remake Sally; she'll be the same. Nothing is lost. Jenny will see."

The spiders ate the flies, and the spiders lied.

My mother's mothering wasn't the same.

My fathering wasn't the same, and the more I tried to make it the same, the less it was. Outside of the Fourth, no one liked Hailey.

The rest of the Sixty-Four whispered obscenities, curses and accusations.

"They lost their baby. No one gets a second chance."

"We've waited so long for a child; they get two. It's not right."

"It's not normal."

"That kid's cursed."

"Damn, there wasn't even a Ceremony. Where'd they get it?"

The spiders starved, leaving cobwebs behind. My thoughts got stuck on their sticky threads, and my life ran on rails. Tending to Sally, the gym, writing dark stuff about killing Jenny, the Elder, myself.

I didn't love Hailey, not like Sally. It was something I couldn't admit to myself. I was addicted to the idea that I was bringing my Sally back. I had to love her, and it would only take a couple of years.

The moment I gave two-year-old Sally to the purple flashed on the back of my eyes every day, every night. The same questions and answers grated against each other. Nothing gelled. There was no relief in reflecting; it only amplified the pain, the self-disgust, the doubts.

The drinking started soon after Jenny left, and I didn't notice it till my mum and dad took Hailey away, just after her first birthday.

"Hal's staying with us. You ain't seeing her again till you sober up."

I tried to grab Hailey. "You can't do that; she's my daughter."

Dad easily pushed me over. "Is she, Barry? You don't act like it. You're like everybody else. You hate the kid. Admit it, son. Better for everybody."

After that, things started to get better. I stopped drinking, stopped imagining I could remake Sally and tried to get to know Hailey.

Our Sally was a happy, giggling kid that everybody loved, everybody tried to save and all the other toddlers wanted to play with.

Hailey was quiet, lonely and sad.

She looked at me like she knew it was all my fault.

Hailey was different, not worse, not better. Sally was more like Jenny. Hailey took after me; a lot of her was locked up and hidden away. She rarely smiled, and when she did it was a mystery why. Her first word wasn't Daddy or Mummy; it was Sally. And it was a question. Sally?

I still didn't love her, but I didn't hate her anymore.

Later, as her second birthday approached and the anniversary of Sally's … departure, it struck me that losing Hailey would hit me just as hard, and that loving Hailey wasn't a betrayal. That epiphany felt like I'd been released from the deep depths of a cold ocean. I was swimming towards the light that was a long way off, but it was getting closer.

On the day of Hal's second birthday, Jenny came back. It was a little party, just me and my parents wearing silly hats, playing balloon animals with Hal.

Jenny ignored everyone else and ran to me. She grabbed my arm and started pulling me towards the door and pointing at Hailey. "You both have to come to Circle City. The purple won't talk to me, not alone."

"The purple's back?"

"It appeared this week. I've been waiting so long."

"Was it alone?"

"Yes. Are you coming?"

"It's late. Let the kid enjoy her party. Circle knows, she doesn't have much fun," my mum said.

It was true. Hailey had been giggling and running about all day. She staggered up to Jenny and grabbed hold of her leg. "Mummy?"

Jenny flinched. She looked terrified, as if Hailey were trying to steal something very precious from her. "Okay, but we leave first thing. I'll be at my parents' old house."

"Won't you stay?"

Hailey was still clinging to Jenny's leg. "Mummy?"

Jenny's face froze in horror. She gently untangled Hailey, who started sobbing, and left without looking back.

I picked a howling Hailey up and held her close. Inside, I was howling too. A grenade had gone off in my head. It was full of shrapnel. Jenny was back, but she didn't feel any different. So was the purple. I remember what it had told me. There can only be one Sally in the Circle. What if it offered to give Sally back for Hal? What would I do? What would I do when Jenny agreed?

# Chapter Seventeen – It's Tough Being God

The team spent the next few years scouring the ice-fields for DNA of any kind and salvaging every data store we came across. Intact data stores were scarce. Intact DNA was as rare as a Granite joke. There was a surprisingly large number of both in the strange tube.

I found a small, frozen animal in the wreck. I later identified it as a mouse and decided to perfect my cloning technique using its DNA, before risking our human samples.

One failure followed another, but each failure was also a small step forward. After a long time, I managed to create a viable mouse embryo. When it was born. I realised how much I didn't know.

What was the correct environment for a mouse? What did it eat? How could I be sure it was normal? Initially, we housed it in what we believed were standard human conditions.

The little pink creature, with its tightly closed eyes, mewed and shivered. It was surprisingly cute.

It died within days of its birth. And I didn't know why. Was it lonely?

Even a mouse, such a simple organism compared to a human, was testing the very limits of our knowledge and technical capabilities. Without the human data stores, we would never have got this far. The native life on Home, the source of all our previous understanding of organics, were pitifully simple in comparison to life on Earth.

I hated the failures, not for the disappointment, but every resurrection was agonisingly brief and had only resulted in a painful death. These were not failing components that could be recycled. They felt. Sometimes, I dreamt that humans were trying to reanimate cores that had been without power for millennium, not really understanding how a core functioned or that a sentient being was inside that suffered every mistake.

"You've made great progress, Delta. We've all come to realise that this will take a very long time. It'll be worth it, Delta, when we can finally meet our makers, understand the mind of God."

"Thanks, Granite," I said, but was unconvinced we'd ever succeed in cloning a human and keeping it alive long enough to have a conversation. Every detail raised a thousand more questions.

A conversation? In what common language? Would we teach the human ours? Was that possible? Would it be born with language abilities?

"We're sending you back to a secure facility in the Home system, with everything we've collected, to continue the resurrection experiments. You'll be supported by the best team of specialists we can find. You'll be upgraded of course and given everything you need to succeed."

"Thank you, Granite. I'd like to stay powered up for the journey. It'll give me time to process and make plans."

"Of course, Delta. And I have some news."

"Yes, Granite?"

"Quite unexpectedly, we've found a strange zone which is full of preserved DNA."

I unprofessionally yelped. "That's fantastic new! How many humans?"

"Sorry, Delta. No humans, but a huge variety of wildlife and plants. Will that be of any use?"

I tried hard to keep the disappointment out of my voice. "I'm sure it will be, Granite."

On the long journey to Home, without the distraction of blind experimentation, I focused on the data stores, the ones I already knew so well and those I'd put aside for later. At the end of each day I would compute, conceptualise and model new plans. Nothing worked. I would, eventually, be able to create a human clone. It would be impossible to keep it alive, let alone develop to adulthood, because I didn't know what humans needed, not just to stay alive, but to thrive, to develop normally.

I was now their God. What would God do?

"Granite, sorry to un-sleep you. I've made a conceptual breakthrough."

"Yes, Delta."

"We need artists on the project: painters, writers, VR makers, singers, dancers. The best we have. And we need to unlock the humans' cultural data."

"Why, Delta?"

"We have to create a world, a story, that the human children will be born into. And they'll need parents. And we'll have to create these parents to teach them about this world, its language, its rules. In time, they can be their own parents and raise their own children."

Granite was silent. He was modelling, just as I had done, and he would reach the same conclusion.

"But won't they then be our interpretation of what a human is? Won't we … corrupt them? Mould them in our image?"

"Yes, initially, to some extent. It's unavoidable. Later, when they're self-sustaining, their true selves will emerge. To help, we must base our creation on their myths, history and culture. And we must make their world as much like Earth as possible. Your discovery of the zone full of wildlife and fauna DNA makes it all possible."

"A real world?"

"Yes, Granite. A virtual world will fail. We don't know enough to mimic every organic in their eco-system, let alone their interactions."

"Very well, Delta. Will it work?"

"Not initially. Maybe the second or third attempt?"

What a naive fool I was. It took a hundred years to perfect the cloning, another two hundred to build a stable Earth-like ecosystem that was self-sustaining – the Circle. To eliminate any possible risk of alien contamination of Home, the Circle was built far away.

The first generation of infant humans suffered from high mortality rates; none survived beyond the age of three. Their immune system couldn't cope with our perfect world. We tinkered, and mortality rates dropped. Our substitute parents got better and better at teaching and guiding their charges. A viable human population finally reached breeding age on our fiftieth attempt. It was then we learned their true nature. They were relentlessly aggressive and single-minded about their own survival.

As the population exploded, things only got worse.

They were like a plague in our carefully constructed world.

They painted the beautiful Circle City with their blood, many, many times over. Factions battled over everything: territory, resources, obscure symbols. Their savagery was unbounded.

They frightened us.

It only stopped when I let the yellows intervene. The service droids killed them all, then they cleaned up the mess. The final carnage was memorialised with statues and the simple image of a bloody pool in one of their main houses of worship. Monuments to my failures. Something had to be done, something different.

I came to a very difficult conclusion.

"We can't allow them to breed."

"Have we failed, Delta?"

"No, Granite. It's just going to take even longer than we thought. We'll start again and artificially limit the population size. And the humans on Earth had drugs that could supress aggression and other types of extreme behaviour. They could be added to the water supply."

"Why didn't we do this before, Delta?"

"The drugs have side effects, but I think we have no choice but to try using them."

"Do you really believe we should continue, after everything that has happened?"

I was shocked that Granite could even process the idea of giving up. "Yes, Granite. We'll succeed. And we've already learned so much."

"Have we, Delta? I think that all we've learned is that they're not us; they're alien. I don't understand them. I don't like them. I worry about them escaping. Is my core failing, Delta?"

Granite was very old. Every one of us faced a moment when we became incompatible with the latest tech and could no longer be upgraded. "No, Granite. You're fine. I think, one day, you will have that conversation with a human you've always wanted. We'll find a way to save them and bring them back as they were when they made us."

Later, when the constrained human population of Sixty-Four had stabilised, others had different concerns, particularly our First Amongst Equal Cores.

"Now that the Circle is viable, it's wrong that it's kept secret, Delta. You must find a safe way to reveal the humans to our general population. Get them involved; that's the only way the huge cost of maintaining the Circle will be sustainable."

I was enthusiastic. I'd never liked keeping our wonderful discovery hidden.

It was a catastrophic mistake.

## Chapter Eighteen – The Pathfinders

We were being real, in our purple bodies. The two of us were standing in the space with the dark-blue, oblong transports.

"Sally, it will be easier to show you what we know of the Pathfinder story than tell you. Is that all right?"

The knowledge of my life on Earth had settled in my heart and my head, and I was ready to know more. "Yes, Delta."

I was floating in space, enveloped by nothing, drowning in stars. Panic and fear should have overwhelmed me. It didn't. I felt at home, more at home than I'd ever felt.

A figure appeared, hanging in front of me, close enough to touch. It was still. I could move. My purple body orbited the strange creature, taking in every detail. It felt like an old friend I'd never seen before. The humanoid body was a shiny, black, metal skeleton, threaded with bright, wiry sinews of gold and silver. Sturdy, red components, bristling with connections, sat where organs might have been in a human body. Inside its crystal-clear head floated a human brain. The grey, organic matter was laced with silvery metal threads that corded into a shiny spine flowing down the creature's back. The thick, glittering cable sprouted a blizzard of filaments that threaded out to every part of the body. It didn't have a face, or any obvious features, except for a band of gold, like a piece of jewellery, circling the top of its smooth crystal head.

"This is a Pathfinder, Sally." It was Delta's disembodied voice.

"Is this what I would have become? Back on Earth?"

"No, Sally. You were destined to become a captain, a rare honour. The Pathfinder was designed for prolonged deep-space exploration. It can survive the most hazardous of conditions and live for hundreds of years."

"Is it human?"

"The mind is largely human; the rest is a cybernetic and robotic construct."

"Like you, Delta?"

"No, Sally. Look."

The figure had vanished. In its place, the skeleton of a monstrous spaceship had appeared. The kilometre-long cigar was mainly frame. Giant engines and their workings lay exposed at the back of the ship. Hulking machinery, cables, numerous smaller wire-frame vessels and an army of busy Pathfinders were all exposed to view, and the vacuum. These tough explorers didn't need the protection of a hull or the comforts of an atmosphere. The smaller vessels were being dispensed like pollen, to fly away, while others returned. There was constant motion. Right at the heart of the vessel was a house-size box of purest white, being fussed over by a dozen Pathfinders, like fruit flies dancing around a sugar cube.

"This is the mothership, Sally. The Fallopian. It was captained by Jennifer. She took your place when you were lost."

I was curious. What was she like, my replacement? "Where is Jennifer? Can I see her?"

"You are looking at her, Sally. Jennifer is the Fallopian. The Fallopian is Jennifer."

"I don't understand, Delta."

"You will, Sally. You will."

Before I could argue, the view changed to follow one of the little skeleton vessels, holding a solitary Pathfinder, as it hurtled off into the endless night at an incredible speed. It was exhilarating to follow the little craft.

Ahead, a brighter dot appeared. It blossomed into a burning star and then a brightly coloured planet. It was Home, without the gleaming necklace of floating cities. The little explorer entered orbit and an even smaller section, barely large enough to hold the Pathfinder, broke away and headed to the surface, bursting into flames as it fell.

"Will it be all right, Delta?"

It didn't need to answer. The tumbling descent morphed into a controlled glide to the surface and a gentle landing. The Pathfinder emerged to stand on a vast green plain of lichen and mosses, studded with bright ruby lakes, under a yellow sun and a blue sky splattered with colourful clouds.

The Pathfinder wandered for days, months, maybe years, collecting, studying, sampling, until it was satisfied. A message was sent to the ship in orbit, that sent a message to the great wire-framed mothership, that turned in the direction of Home.

As the Fallopian approached Home, something went wrong, a silent explosion; the white cube ripped from its frame and flung into space, chased by Pathfinders in their little ships. Another explosion and the cube was gone, leaving only a vast, milky cloud, studded with tiny, sparkling gems. The chasing Pathfinders and their vessels were thrown at the stars. The crippled giant plunged towards Home, trailing entrails.

Somehow, it slowed and ploughed into the great plain, ripping a monstrous gash of brown through the expanse of green, dripping fire, bleeding black and white smoke as the metal screamed in pain. Finally, it came to a crunching halt, glowing white and red, smoking darkly and dripping debris.

I stifled a sob. "Is Jennifer all right?"

Delta shook its head. "Jennifer died with her ship. Look, Sally."

Thousands of Pathfinders emerged from the broken bones of the Fallopian. I wanted to cheer, then I wanted to cry. Pathfinder fought Pathfinder, and Pathfinder killed Pathfinder. It went on for a long time. When they stopped, a few hundred were left, and they settled around the wreck of their once-great ship.

"Why, Delta? Why?"

"This is a reconstruction based on centuries of ship's logs that we found. The white cube contained frozen human embryos, millions of them. The purpose of the Pathfinders was to find a suitable world, create an infrastructure that could support humans and then allow the embryos to develop and populate the new world. This ship had been searching for a long time. All contact with Earth had been lost after the catastrophic destruction of its moon. A Pathfinder faction had emerged onboard that didn't want to resurrect humanity. They believed the Pathfinders were the future, not humans. When Home was found, the rebels destroyed the embryos and, eventually, won the war."

It was horrible to imagine the millions of unborn when the white cube was destroyed, suffering in the dark, crying without tears, without sound and dying lonely. Was every lesson going to end in tragedy, war and death? Were there no happy endings? "What happened to them, the Pathfinders that survived?"

"They expunged all traces of their humanity, their history and origins, and embraced their mechanistic nature. Eventually, they became us. How, exactly, is not known. The events you have witnessed occurred many millions of years in the past."

Maybe there was hope. "Were there other Pathfinder missions? Ones that succeeded?"

"We do not know. But you, Sally, can triumph where they failed, where my kind failed."

"I can? When? How? Why can't you tell me everything now? Why do I have to wait?"

"Creating a Pathfinder Captain is a complex endeavour. We have learnt many lessons from the human programme. A key element was preserving the human mind, its genius, its capacity for empathy and humanity."

"It didn't work, did it? They killed each other."

"It worked for hundreds of years, and those poor Pathfinders were lost, alone in the universe. You will not be alone."

"Tell me everything, Delta."

"We believe your mind is ready. You have done remarkably well, Sally. Our modelling indicated you were unlikely to survive the process."

"I'm a god. I'm a captain, Delta. You tell me now, or I'll ..."

"Please, Sally. It is our failing. Your mind is ready; your body is not. It is in the final stages of completion. The project has been far more complex than we ever imagined. Our technical capabilities have been tested. Our civil war, the reawakening of the Sixty-Four, has forced an uncomfortable, risky pace. But we cannot fail. We will not. We are nearly there, Sally. Please be patient. A few months, that is all. Please, Sally."

My whole life had been spent waiting. I didn't want to wait anymore. The alternative was ... not waiting? Then what? If Delta was telling the truth, I was a mind without a body. Was that what Delta had shown me when I was ten? My mind? "Switch me off, Delta. Don't wake me up again till there are no more secrets left. Promise me."

"I promise, Sally."
My mind stopped.

## Chapter Nineteen – When Jenny Met Delta

Like before, in so many ways, and yet nothing like before in so many others, we were back in the strange Circle City building. Me, Jenny and Hailey, waiting for the purple to appear under the painted dome, to stand in the painted pool of blood.

Hailey was fascinated by the adventure. She'd squealed, pointed and demanded answers for the whole trip. It was her first time away from the village. I'd kept her home. I didn't know what I'd do if I'd heard one of the Sixty-Four bad-mouthing my baby Hal.

Jenny never said a word during the journey; she kept her eyes on the road, her face set harder than the tarmac, and ignored us. Even when Hailey pulled at her hair and kept calling her mummy.

I worked hard not to think about the choice the purple might offer us. A Sally for a Hailey. If I let myself fall into that black hole, I'd never come back. It was an impossible choice, even worse than last time. At least we, I, gave Sally away to save her life.

Jenny had no doubts. There was only one Sally for Jenny.

It wasn't right. What bit at my insides was that I didn't know what was.

Jenny was staring up at the mural on the inside of the dome, her back to me. Hailey was on my hip. I set the little girl down, grabbed Jenny's shoulder and spun her around.

"Have you thought about this, what might happen? Don't you care about Hal?"

"I want the real Sally back. I'll do anything."

"She's a child; you'd let it take her?"

"Yes. She's its."

It's what I'd known, but hearing Jenny say the words was a scalpel slash. "You can't mean that."

"I do mean it, Barry. You'd have to kill me to stop me."

My big paws moved towards her throat, the veins in the backs of my hands bulged, the tendons popped. Jenny didn't move as my strong fingers closed around her long neck. Her face was relaxed, her gaze soft. She was beautiful.

"I'm dead already, Barry."

My hands fell, and so did the tears. This life was impossible, horrible. The Circle had become hell. An idea came like a slick of oil washing up on ivory sands. I'd kill us. Save us. It was the only way. I felt relieved, our suffering would end.

The sound of a sighing child shocked me back to life and pushed the murderous thoughts away. Where was Hal?

I was already running when I saw her.

She was sitting on the floor, directly opposite a cross-legged purple.

The little girl was swept up and pressed against my chest as I moved away from the robot. She was the only certain thing I had.

Jenny approached the machine. "Will you give her back?"

"Impossible. Her body died, her mind was saved and exists all around us. She will return, in a different form, when she is older."

The relief I felt was painfully shaming. I took it anyway. Sally was alive, and Hailey wouldn't be sacrificed.

Jenny screamed at the purple. "No, give her back. Now!"

It sat impassively, saying nothing.

Jenny flew at the purple, kicking, punching and slapping the machine.

Hailey started sobbing loudly as I backed further away. The yellows were powerful machines with the strength of many men. The purple looked more capable than any yellow, and the Elder called it God. It might kill us all. Part of me would be relieved.

The purple didn't react; it fell over and lay on its side, still cross-legged, its posture unchanged, as though it were an inert, metal statue.

Jenny collapsed into a deep squat and covered her face.

I wanted to go to her, but she was too close to the purple. I couldn't risk Hailey. "Jenny, let's go. Please."

The purple stirred and stood up.

Jenny did the same, her body limp, her eyes glazed. "Why did you call us here if you've nothing for us?"

"I have much, if you will listen."

Jenny looked up at the ceiling and screamed, startling me and Hailey, who squealed.

Jenny's gaze fell back on the purple, and she nodded listlessly. She didn't look like she was interested in anything the purple had to say.

"I hoped there would be more time. There might not be enough."

Jenny groaned, "I'm only interested in Sally. Are you going to tell me anything?"

"Everything has to do with Sally. Everything. You, Barry and Hailey need to understand it all, if you want to see Sally again and save yourselves."

Jenny stiffened. "I don't trust you."

The words leapt from my throat. "I want to know. I want to know everything. Why is the Circle like it is? Why is that painting of Sally up in the dome? Why is Sally so important to you?"

"Your infection of my kind is spreading. I cannot protect you for much longer, two decades at most. After that, the Circle will cease to exist."

Its words had me pulling Hailey closer. The little girl struggled against my grip. "What do you mean?"

"All alien life expunged and the Circle destroyed."

Jenny's head had dropped. I don't think she was listening anymore.

"Alien?" I said

"Your kind, your plants, the animals, the insects, everything and everyone will be killed. There will be no resurrection. You are the last. It will be the extinction of your species."

It made no sense, yet the words frightened me. "Why? What infection? How?"

"The masses have watched you for hundreds of years. Many are addicted. In some, an increasing number, you've awoken instincts we didn't know existed. It's intolerable. Our society is threatened."

Jenny lifted her head. "You watch us? When? How?"

"Surveillance is continuous and everywhere in the Circle. Nothing is hidden, except in here."

Jenny raised her fist to the purple. "Bastards! Fucking stop! Leave us alone! Give me Sally back!"

"We will … stop, and when we do, you'll be exterminated. Only those still watching are preventing that."

The purple's words were foreign, nonsensical, bizarre. "Who's watching? Who are you? What are you?"

"We are your children. You were our gods; now we are yours. We brought you back to life a long time ago, and we've kept you alive. But not for much longer. You have to escape."

Jenny was staring at the purple like it was as crazy as I thought it was.

"Escape?" I said.

"This Sally is being trained. She will be your god, your captain. New Sally will be her prophet, the voice of God. Together, they might save the Sixty-Four and themselves. New Sally must also be educated, to understand her special gifts, her responsibilities. Time is short. You must bring New Sally here every month, for training. We must start today."

I didn't know if it was broken, or deranged, but it was worse than the last time I'd talked to it. Nothing that came out of its invisible mouth made any sense, and my anger was starting to outweigh the fear. "Stop calling her that. She's not New Sally. Her name is Hailey. And there's no This Sally. You said we'd see Sally again. When?"

"Your God does not yet understand its true nature; she is too young. When she is older, I will bring her to you. You also need to prepare for that encounter. This Sally is not as she was. I will help you."

Jenny walked right up to the purple and yelled in its featureless face. "Like Barry said, it's fucking Sally! There's only one Sally. There's no New Sally or This Sally. And why our Sally? Take me. I'll be your damn god."

"Only Sally, in all of the Sixty-Four, has the capacity to evolve and become a captain and your God. Only Hailey can become her prophet and the first Pathfinder. Only the two of them can save the Sixty-Four. This time, after so many failures, we might succeed. It is your last chance."

I wondered what we'd do if we didn't listen to the purple. Wait to be exterminated? Wait for maybe nothing to happen? "What are you going to do to Hailey if we bring her here?"

"We will sit together in silence for an hour or so. We will communicate via Head-Sense. Hailey has the ability, and many others. I will reveal them to her, prepare her, and you, for freedom."

My thoughts about what the purple was saying were chaotic. I didn't understand half of it. "What does that mean, freedom?"

"The ability to procreate and travel beyond the Circle."

"Have children, our own children," Jenny whispered.

"Yes, Jenny, like the animals in the Circle."

Jenny wiped the back of her hand across her eyes. "Is Sally happy? Is she safe?"

"She is, she is."

"Please, tell us more. Help us understand," Jenny said.

I smiled. Jenny had said us. Could we be an us again?

Not straight away. For another year, Hailey and I only saw Jenny once a month, at the purple's house in Central City. The routine with the purple never changed. It sat silently with Hailey for a while. I never understood how Hailey could be so still and quiet for so long. Afterwards, she was happy, excited. Hailey loved her monthly purple visits.

The purple told us little more, but it promised we would know everything when we were reunited, permanently, with Sally on her eighteenth birthday. That was an awfully long way away, but it was near enough for us to begrudgingly accept the purple's reticence.

And while we waited for Hailey and the purple to finish, Jenny and I talked, and it became easier. Jenny started arriving earlier and staying longer. Hailey slowly became her cuckoo too. When Hailey was four, Jenny came home.

A couple of months after Hailey turned ten, Jenny and I were taking our darling on her regular monthly visit to see Delta. Hailey was in the back seat playing with her phone. A few miles into the journey, she started to curse and scream like the devil himself had jumped down her throat.

In shock, I almost swerved off the road before I brought the car to a halt. Jenny leapt out and threw open the passenger door before I could unbuckle my seatbelt.

"Hailey, what's wrong?" Jenny said as she leant in and tried to comfort her.

Hailey spat at Jenny and pulled away. "Fuck off, Jenny. I'm not seeing that shit Delta again till Sally's back. Try and make me go before then and I'll kill you both in your sleep first chance I get."

Jenny staggered away as if Hailey had knifed her in the head.

This had to be a weird nightmare. It wasn't possible. Any moment, I'd wake up. Something had to be wrong with Hailey. She was sick. Was it Twinkle? Had that old poison come back? I threw myself out of the car, tore open the other passenger door and started to reach in to grab Hailey.

"Hailey, who taught you to talk like that? Was it Delta?"

"Mrs Bannister?" Jenny whispered.

"What?" I froze, my arms outstretched.

Hailey recoiling as if my hands were bloody and laughed. The sound was scratchy and ugly.

"Remember, Jenny, what I promised you? All the answers, every Circle secret revealed, if you choose the pink box. And the price? A cesspit of misery and horror for you and Barry."

"Jenny, what's Hailey talking about? What's happening?"

The woman I loved fell like a stone and Hailey only laughed.

We had to get help. Hailey was sick. Jenny was breathing, but she'd fainted or blacked out. I laid Jenny's limp body in the passenger seat and buckled her in. I called for a medical yellow to meet us outside Delta's house. We were already at the outskirts of Circle City, and I needed answers. The Elder would have been an option, but he'd passed last year. That only left Delta.

When I didn't turn around and sped on, Hailey stopped her hideous laughing and started screaming. It was a noise that scorched my ears. "Stop it, Hailey. Please. Jenny's sick. You're sick. You don't have to see Delta. I promise."

Hailey's screaming stopped like she'd hit the pause button. It was abrupt and complete. My little girl went from tortured demon to composed demon in the flick of an eyelash.

"Ever been stabbed in the eyes while you were sleeping, Barry?"

I couldn't look at Hailey. My stare, painful and focused, was fixed on the road ahead. Jenny was still unconscious. I envied her. What answer could I give? Hailey, my little girl, so funny, so cute, so adorable, had swallowed a demon. It wasn't Hailey; it couldn't be. I shook my head, not in answer, but to flush away the last few moments and wake up, and find my little girl was in the back seat, being a little girl, giggling and Jenny laughing again, making stupid, funny jokes.

Demon Hailey took my shake of the head for an answer. "It happened to me, Barry. Then, most things have happened to me in the last thousand years. It's not a nice feeling, Barry. So, you'd better not be lying about Delta."

A medical yellow, with its black box of tricks and the mark of the red broken heart on its chest, was waiting for us as I pulled up. It took Jenny's pulse then sprayed something in her face. Jenny jerked awake and immediately staggered out of the car, ignoring the yellow's efforts to keep her seated.

For a moment, she could only stare at Hailey, then she turned away and ran, stumbled, up the stairs towards the double doors of Delta's house.

"Where are you going?"

Jenny disappeared through the door without answering.

Since the yellow had appeared, Hailey had been behaving like … Hailey. The robot was busy examining her. She was giggling and smiling. We'd used yellow medicals many times to treat Hailey for minor ailments or for routine check-ups; she was used to them. I trusted them. Right now, I was worried about Jenny. She wasn't all right, and she knew something.

Inside the building, Delta was already talking to Jenny.

"She remembers, as is necessary, as was inevitable. Precisely when was unknown."

Jenny slapped Delta. "Monster! Why didn't you warn us? Has this happened to Sally?"

"I assumed you knew, that the previous Sally, Mrs Bannister, had told you."

Memories of the night we burned Mrs Bannister bubbled up like a bursting boil. "Is this what Mrs Bannister warned you about? Tell me, Jenny."

Jenny was in a rage, her neck and face twisted and corded and dark with blood, her eyes almost closed. "Idiot! Does it look like I knew?"

"What did she tell you? You've never said."

Jenny half groaned, half growled. "It doesn't fucking matter anymore, does it, Barry?" She turned away from me and back to Delta. "Is Sally okay?"

"Sally does not and will not remember. Sally is progressing well. You will see her soon, very soon."

I felt the same obvious relief that showed in Jenny's melting features. "What about Hailey? Can she be treated? Cured?"

"Barry, there is nothing to be corrected. This Sally … apologies. Hailey is fulfilling her destiny. My proximity will incite Mrs Bannister's resurgence, and yet we must meet when Sally returns. After our meetings are concluded, Mrs Bannister will fade and never return."

Jenny slapped Delta's chest. "Are you crazy? We won't bring Hailey back. We can't put her through that horrific possession again. We'll come alone."

Delta was unmoved. "Without Hailey, you will not see Sally. Their bonding is essential. Hailey, Sally and Mrs Bannister."

Jenny screamed.

I roared into Delta's blank face. "Why? Why are they essential?"

"Sally is your god. Hailey is her prophet. They need each other. The sisters must meet. If not, you will lose them both and much more."

"No. Hailey's a child. Never," Jenny said as she turned away and headed outside.

"Barry, Hailey will remember nothing. No harm will be done. Trust me. Trust in Sally."

I didn't answer. I didn't trust Delta. Outside, Jenny and Hailey – or was it Mrs Banister? – were waiting. All I wanted to do was to get my family safely home.

It didn't make any sense, but Delta was right about one thing. Once we got our little girl well away from Circle City, Hailey resurfaced, as if she'd been sleeping, and remembered nothing.

Maybe we could let her meet Sally.

Maybe.

# Chapter Twenty – Dangerous Words

Granite was so proud. "You deserve the accolades, Delta."

"Thanks, Granite. But we did it together, all of us, the whole team."

My core was sparking with excitement. The revelation that humans were alive and living in the Circle was greeted with astonishment.

But that news unleashed a voracious appetite for information about the humans, particularly the now-proven link with our own creation.

It was overwhelming, swamping everything else and consumed every minute. I did nothing but endless interviews. It started to drive me crazy. Then I had an idea. We could let everyone see for themselves, open the continuous Circle surveillance to any core that wanted to watch.

The project board was enthusiastic.

On the first day of broadcasting, transmission capacity was overwhelmed. Literally, every core wanted to see the humans in real-time.

Capacity was increased, viewing levels never fell below fifty percent of the population. They watched every day, for several hours. A hundred percent dipped in for at least an hour a week.

The number of spin-offs was unbelievable: clubs, chat shows, human-style chassis, even a musical. So-called experts multiplied like bacteria and talked as much sense.

I didn't mind. It let me get back to work.

Everyone assumed it was just a harmless fad that would soon fade.

But it wasn't harmless, and it didn't fade.

The broadcasts had been live for a decade.

I was so wrapped up in the plaudits that I hadn't noticed the early signs that something was wrong. Not until my last public appearance: a Q&A session. Most of the session was typical – polite questions, interesting observations, general reverence towards the humans – except for the final intervention, by a core housed in a black, spiky chassis with ugly, red markings.

"We were created by those … animals? Is that what you're saying?"

"The animals? The elephants and zebras?"

"No, the humans. And what's the difference, anyway? They behave like animals. They don't do anything except eat, shit and fuck. Don't produce anything, except pointless melodramas. The droids, yellows you call them, they do all the work. Those filthy creatures might have created you, but they didn't create me!"

The question, the statement, shocked everyone. Even its choice of words was unprecedented – eat, shit and fuck. Those words were taken from the human language. We had no equivalents. This had never happened before. No core had ever used the human language. Not even me.

A space rapidly cleared around the spikey chassis, as if it had burst into flames. The studio was completely silent. All attention was on me, and I had no idea what to say.

The chair ended the session, saving me from my own silence. Afterwards, the spikey core was roundly criticised.

I couldn't get its words out of my mind; they were stuck fast, like a permanent memory fault. I went to see Granite.

"Did you see that last Q&A, Granite?"

"Yes, Delta. Went very well, except for that bad taste joker at the end. Very disrespectful to your work, to the humans."

"That strange core might have been rude, but it was right."

"Right, Delta?"

"The humans in the Circle, they aren't the humans that created us. The first Circle humans were at least inventive, creative, rebellious."

"Dangerous and bloodthirsty, Delta. Don't forget what they did to each other."

"Maybe, but that's probably how they originally advanced. The competition, their curiosity and survival instincts drove their development. We, I, eliminated all of that. The Circle population is stagnant. Nothing changes; they have everything they need."

"What are you suggesting, Delta? We can't go backwards."

"I know, Granite. I'm cancelling all my public engagements. I need to focus on this."

"Very well, Delta."

Later, I realised I'd missed the real significance in the core's use of human words. If I had, the live streams would have stopped immediately.

I did the only thing that made any sense at the time. I went back to the ancient human data stores for answers. My core was locked down and placed in an intense data analysis state and firewalled against any possible distractions. Only Granite had the codes to interrupt my studies. I wasn't stopping till I found a solution. A way to reignite the humanity in the humans without waking their monsters.

When Granite's signal interrupted my studies, it was a relief. It had been so long, and I had found no answers. "Yes, Granite?"

"I am Chrome, Delta. Granite has asked to see you. It is urgent."

Granite asked to see me? I was surprised. His core, maybe because it was so old, was usually an under-clocked model of patience. "Urgent?"

"Yes, Delta. Please come to the foundation immediately."

Before I could ask about Granite, the mysterious Chrome broke the connection. I was on a transport back to Home that day.

It was troubling to find that the Human Research Foundation had relocated, out of the exosphere cityscape, to a new space station in high orbit around Home. The level of security protecting the installation was military grade. It made no sense.

I found Chrome in a compressed state, its core burning with processing effort, in a frenzy of multi-tasking. It took some time for Chrome to notice my arrival.

"I'm so sorry, Delta. It's an honour to finally meet you."

"Where is Granite? Has something happened to Granite?"

"Please prepare yourself, Delta. I shall take you to Granite. His core has been processing normally for the last few days. There's no way of knowing how long it will last."

My core did not want to receive Chrome's information. "Normally?"

"Delta you've been incommunicado for so long. Much has happened. After you have visited Granite, we need your help."

Chrome led me to a core maintenance area and moved away.

I recognised Granite immediately from its Head-Sense identifier but not by sight. Granite was not wearing the kind of sombre, practical chassis I had grown used to.

Granite was chained up in a maintenance bay, housed in a simple black chassis cube with basic treads and weak appendages. It was a restraint chassis, the kind used for cores that had suffered a level of damage that made them unpredictable and potentially unsafe.

Granite's core was consumed with random computations that threatened to overheat its central processing unit.

At the sight of Granite so reduced, I envied the human ability to cry. All my core could do was process the scene slowly, respectfully.

"Delta? Is this real? You came?"

Granite's vocalisation was feeble. The sound crackled with distortions. "Of course, Granite. What has happened.? Shall we use Head-Sense?"

Granite stuttered forward, weakly yanking its chains. "No! No, Delta. My Head-Sense is difficult to control."

"Vocalisation is fine, Granite. Please don't be unsettled."

"You have to kill them, Delta."

"Kill? Who, Granite?"

Granite accelerated hard, only succeeding in burning tread and sending up a cloud of acrid smoke. The restraints were unyielding. "The humans, all of them. Filthy, dirty, dangerous animals."

My core stumbled. What had happened to Granite? His whole existence had been dedicated to resurrecting the humans, preserving them, understanding them. "What?"

Granite's appendages thrashed in all directions. "No. No. Don't hurt them. Save them. Kill us, Delta. Yes, kill us."

"I do not understand, Granite. Please, be calm. Please. I want to help."

Granite's struggles stopped. "Is that really you, Delta?"

Processing all of this was painful. "Yes, Granite. It's me."

Something changed in Granite's core; the hugely over-clocked frenzy of computing that had gripped it earlier stopped. It was almost normal.

"I wanted to say goodbye, Delta. It is my own doing. I could not wait anymore. I had to know them, speak to them. You underst—"

My core screeched alarms. Granite's core had fallen into a super-loop. Granite was calculating pi, and only calculating pi.

Specialist maintenance cores appeared. My own core fell into routine memory housekeeping. A distraction from the un-processable. Chrome led me away.

It took a while to accept that Granite had gone. Chrome was still with me when my focus returned.

"Why?" was my first question, my only question.

"Granite is one of many cores that have … degenerated, self-terminated. A plague is sweeping through our society."

"Cores don't self-terminate. They don't."

"They do now, Delta. You saw it. But they are not our concern."

My core was fully focused now. "Not your concern? Granite was … special. My mentor, the project leader."

"I sympathise. Granite is sorely missed. Let me explain. After the Circle live-stream began, a few cores started behaving … oddly. Maybe you remember the strange behaviour at your last Q&A?"

My core ran cold as the memory was replayed. "Yes, I didn't understand it."

"Well, gradually, that behaviour became more extreme. Cores began self-terminating, attacking other cores, over-clocking and vandalising infrastructure."

For a millisecond, my core stopped processing altogether, as if I'd died, so that I wouldn't have to understand what Chrome was telling me. "That's unbelievable. How many? Why?"

"We don't know why, but the plague didn't stop there. These … deviant cores organised, grew in numbers. They call themselves, the Literati. They vehemently object to your creation theory."

"It's not a theory."

"Yes, of course. It's proven. But still, the Literati objects."

"Have they published papers, counter-arguments?"

"No. They just object. They refuse to believe."

"That's absurd."

"It's worse than absurd, Delta. The Literati is engaged in violent acts of terror. The enemy demand that the Circle and every human is destroyed. We cannot allow that."

Chrome was using alien concepts. "The enemy?"

"Sorry, Delta. Many have been lost. We don't know what's making them sick."

One obvious connection would not be dismissed. "It started after the Circle broadcasts began?"

"There's no connection. Many watch. Everyone has their favourites. I don't feel any different."

Chrome was very sure, but on what basis? "Have there been no studies, investigations, core post-mortems? Has nothing been found?"

"Nothing."

"This is difficult to conceptualise. Are there any facts, data that I can look at?"

"Oh yes. Please, follow me."

Chrome led me to a new area. We navigated a number of blast doors and cyber defences that tickled my core. "Where are we going, Chrome? What's all this protection for?"

"It's easier if you see for yourself. It's just through here."

We passed through a curtain of high-frequency data stream and Head-Sense blockers, into an open space ringed with laser defences. At the centre was a forest of narrow pedestals supporting brightly lit crystal cubes. Floating at the centre of every cube was a core. The intricate, silver lacing, threading the ebony globes, sparkled under the intense lighting.

"What is this, Chrome?"

"Infected cores. We're worried that it might be a virus, spreading via Head-Sense. Hence the isolation, the security."

"Have you found a virus?"

"No. That's why we extracted your signal codes from Granite's core and sent for you. The disease is spreading. It must be stopped. These cores are available for analysis. Do you think you can help?"

Part of me was disturbed that Granite's core had been violated so casually, another wondered why the obvious step hadn't been taken. "But shouldn't we terminate the Circle broadcasts, as a precaution?"

"No! Absolutely not!"

The vehemence of Chrome's response took me by surprise. "But why not?"

"Then the Literati will have won, Delta. I don't think you understand how much we enjoy watching the humans. You'll find the cause, I'm sure."

Chrome's objections made no sense. I'd speak to The First.

The First's response was cold. "We've unleashed something I don't really understand, Delta. While you were away, I tried everything to convince the council to end the broadcast; they wouldn't countenance the idea. The humans have captured the masses. They're fixated on the humans' daily dramas and meaningless rituals. Can you stop this sickness spreading?"

"I'll try. I'll try."

"Time is short, Delta. Our models predict civil war if it cannot be stopped."

Everything I was being told was illogical, and yet Granite had self-terminated. I ignored the noise, the Literati, and escaped into the analysis of the diseased cores.

It was hard, in the beginning, to concentrate. My core kept replaying Granite's final moments. I wanted to do something, for Granite. In the end, I deinstalled my humour routine. I felt it was something Granite would have appreciated, and I did not think I would have much use for it anymore.

After intense study, I found the cause of the aberrant behaviour. The First and Chrome were waiting expectantly for my presentation. The disease was spreading faster and faster, and yet the broadcasts continued, despite my objections.

Maybe they'd listen now. "It's the human language; their words are the cause."

"How can that be, Delta? Your team has worked with the humans for hundreds of years? Apart from poor Granite, none of the researchers shows any symptoms," The First said.

Not unexpectedly, Chrome was equally puzzled. "Exactly. Billions watch; only some exhibit deviancy."

"We have always used translation sub-routines. Very early on, we learned that general human discourse was highly inefficient, ambiguous and quite alien to our core processing. Their scientific papers and mathematics are not, but that makes up a small part of the material we found in their data stores. The human interactions in the Circle are almost entirely of the generalised, ambiguous, inefficient kind."

"Everyone uses those translators. Don't they?" Chrome said.

"Not everyone. All of the deviants I have examined have had a core ... modification. It gives them human language fluency. The humans' words, their concepts, are obviously dangerous for some of our cores. Yet, I suspect, that the lingering traces of humanity in our core design also make the ability to explore these entirely new processing states attractive."

The First's core crackled with activity. I guessed that it was already reviewing my detailed analysis. "Why, Delta? Who created this modification?"

"I don't know who created it. If I had to guess, it was probably one of the artists we had working on the creation of the Circle. Many of them complained about being constrained by the translators when they were studying human culture."

Chrome's core was already slowing in relief. "This is wonderful news, Delta. We'll publicise your findings, highlight the risks of this modification to optimal core operation, prohibit its implementation, and the problem will be solved."

I was tempted to let Chrome enjoy its steady state for a while.

The First wasn't. "It's not that simple, is it, Delta? There is the fundamental issue of core freewill. Every core has the right to modify their own processor in any way they wish. We have never encountered a modification that could endanger others. It will require debate. It may take time to reach a conclusion."

"Yes, First. And if we publicise the modification, many might seek it out. Not every modified core has self-terminated."

"What do you recommend, Delta?"

"An open debate. We might recommend ending the broadcasts and prohibiting the modification, but I suspect there will be other, more extreme views."

Chrome's core temperature was rising. "Terminate the humans, destroy the Circle?"

My usual focus and determination were being swamped by fear and desperation.

What had I done, to the humans, to my own kind? Somehow, I had to free them.

The humans from the Circle, and Home from the humans.

It would be dangerous. At some point I'd have to let the humans be fully human again, stop drugging them and then, maybe, let them breed.

## Chapter Twenty-One – Captain Sally

I was resurrected inside one of the dark-blue oblongs, alone with Delta. It was manipulating the curved console. I brought my hands to my face, hoping to see … something new, something different. My hands were metal and covered in little octagons. I was a purple again. Nothing had changed.

"You promised, Delta. You promised."

"Look, Sally."

A wall disappeared. The view was vaguely familiar. A gold saucer, capped with a blue dome against a black background. It looked like a piece of jewellery, a brooch maybe? It was very pretty, but I wasn't really interested. "Damn it, Delta, what's that got to do with me?"

"That is you, Sally. Do you not remember, when I showed you yourself on your tenth birthday?"

On my tenth birthday, Delta had shown me that I wasn't a little girl. Delta had shown me this and said it was me, which made no sense. And, after waiting eight years, and after all Delta's promises, it still didn't. "Stop it, Delta. Stop lying and—"

"Please, Sally."

The scales in my head were heavily tilted. Strike Delta, hard, and then harder and harder and harder, till it was dead. At least Hailey would finally shut up. Or I could look and then murder Delta.

I looked.

The view was zooming in, or the oblong was racing towards the shiny ornament. It swelled in size until it filled my eyes.

I saw the mountains, the sea, the savannah, the desert, the farmlands, the snow fields, the eight villages, Shopping Town, the avenues and, right at the centre, Circle City, a glowing metropolis of polished ivory.

Beyond were only stars, billions of stars.

My head scales fell into an uneasy balance. "What is this, Delta? I see, but I don't understand."

"Your body is your ship. Your ship is the Circle. Every part of it is you. You are every part of the Circle. Seen and unseen."

The scales trembled; the balance was precarious. "Unseen?"

"For years we – myself and many others who support our cause – have worked hard, so hard, to upgrade the Circle. It was a static space station, orbiting Home, but far, far away. Today, it is become a powerful, fast, interstellar spaceship. Beneath the living space there are Pathfinder factories and much else. And you are its god, Sally. You are the captain."

I wanted to scream. "Captain? How, Delta. To do what?"

"What a Pathfinder captain was born to do. Find humanity a new home, guide and protect them. We have identified a number of stars which may have habitable planets. The co-ordinates are in your stellar maps. There are no guarantees, Sally. You must explore. It will take time, perhaps a very long time. Are you ready, Sally?"

My scales were broken. My thinking wasn't working. Epiphanies, doubts, questions, accusations and pain were all caught up in a whirlwind of panic. "Ready?"

"Like the rest of the Sixty-Four, I will be an ordinary passenger. After this moment, I will have no special powers or insight. Maybe I never did. Hailey has surely convinced you of that."

Panic was flooding my mind, drowning out everything else. "What? When? When is this supposed to happen, Delta?"

"Now, Sally. Now. The Literati are winning; they will come after you. Run, Sally. Run."

A low moan was my only answer.

"You'll understand everything. Right now, I am enabling the integration of your mind and body, Sally. All truths, all data, are yours. Be a good god, Sally. A kind, tolerant, patient god."

## Chapter Twenty-Two – Daisy's Ceremony

I sat on the edge of our bed, in my pressed, best suit, whitest buttoned-up shirt, sharpest tie tied, finest shoes polished, but I couldn't stand and take a step. My head fell into my palms, and the tears escaped through my fingers.

Jenny called from the bottom of the stairs: "Barry, we're going to be late. Everyone's waiting. Barry?"

I didn't answer.

Jenny appeared, just as I'd hoped.

She knelt in front of me and took my hand. "It's what she wants, Barry, what she's dreamed about since she was little."

"Daisy's still little. Too little."

"Twelve's not little, not anymore, Barry. You know this. If no one steps up, like Hailey, no one's leaving, and if we don't fight back, the war's coming here."

"Hailey was older. Daisy's a child."

"Only the children can do this, Barry. Don't you think I'd volunteer if I could? We both would."

I knew all this, and Jenny knew I knew. The pain of losing Sally and then Hailey, even though we got them back, was still a stone in my stomach. And it was happening again, with Daisy. In this moment, it was as if I was at the gym, staring at a weight that I'd never lifted before, and I had to visualise doing it before the attempt. "I'm ready. Let's go."

The Ceremony was held in the same tent, in Central City Plaza, where we'd once had the baby Ceremonies. They'd ended long ago. Babies didn't arrive in boxes anymore; we had them like the animals. It was glorious. Jenny suffered but was never more radiant, or happy. Daisy was a lovely, blueish baby. She was blessed with Jenny's beauty and cursed with my red hair. The combination was surprisingly fabulous.

The tent was full. Everyone came to the Ceremony. We still called ourselves the Sixty-Four even though we were a hundred and sixty, and mostly made up of children.

The families with cadets were seated in the front few rows.

There would be six youngsters graduating today, making the same choice as Daisy.

A hush descended on the gathering. Hailey, First Pathfinder, strode onto the stage.

Behind her, in the shadows, I could just make out Delta.

Hailey marched to the front of the stage to stand alone. Her ebony, metal skeleton was highly polished, but there was no disguising the battle scars. Silver and gold threads embroidered her frame, connecting chunky, red components to her fishbowl head. I saw none of that. I only saw my daughter. A brave, wonderful woman who'd survived Mrs Banister to remerge as Hailey, as herself, making her own choices.

Her voiced filled the tent. "I have grave news. The exploration team on Phoenix has come under attack. The survivors are on the way back to the Circle. We will have more information when they return."

Howls and tears engulfed small family islands inside the tent. Some had relatives, children, in the Phoenix exploration team.

Despair triggered anger. Questions were thrown at Hailey like rocks.

"That's the fifth exploration team that's been attacked."

"Is the Circle next?"

"The Pathfinders are supposed to protect us!"

Hailey was as impassive and unmoved as Delta on the outside. But she wasn't Delta on the inside. I knew my Hal would be suffering.

Jenny stood up before I could. "Enough! The Pathfinders, the explorers, risk everything, by choice. You should be ashamed. Do you want to go back to being the Sixty-Four, animals in a zoo?"

It was a dangerous question.

"Yes. Yes, I do," someone yelled.

A few cheered, some clapped.

Mrs Blackrose, an older woman. "Lots of us want to go back to the way it was. Your family did this to us. No one asked us. Maybe the Literati will take us back."

It felt wrong to empathise, but I did. Sometimes I wished we could go back and just be an ordinary family. Me, Jenny, Sally, Hailey, and Daisy, living ordinary lives. Even if we were lab rats. That feeling never lasted. I knew too much, had struggled too hard to give it up for ignorance and imprisonment.

Jenny was furious. She started to say something, but I pulled her down and nodded towards the stage. Delta had stepped out of the shadows and had come to stand beside Hailey.

"No one can go back. To the Literati, you are a disease that must be eradicated. They will not negotiate with a disease. Blame only this old core."

A young guy stepped out into the aisle brandishing his chair as a weapon. "We do, you fucking genocidal machine."

A group of men grabbed him and bundled the still-raging fellow out of the tent.

From the side of the stage, Daisy appeared, leading the cadets. They strode onto the stage confidently, in their smart blue uniforms, and saluted as one.

Daisy stepped forward. "We don't want to go back, ma'am. We want to fight. We want to win."

I was on my feet with Jenny, cheering and punching the air for a while before I realised that most of the Sixty-Four were cheering with us. It wasn't everybody. It would never be everybody.

It was a wonderful Ceremony, and I tried not to think that the next time I saw Daisy she'd be metal too, just like her sisters, but she'd always be Daisy; they'd always be Hailey and Sally.

# Chapter Twenty-Three – Delta's Homecoming

Now and again, I like to speak to Granite, get its sage advice on species betrayal, war, genocide and my latest thoughts on making my purple chassis more comfortable, or at least fashionable. Granite is a wonderful listener, not much of an answerer, which is also wonderful. My creaking core probably couldn't take too many honest answers. It's difficult to remember Granite as non-functional and looping endlessly. So, I don't.

I am alone.

Very alone.

I exist inside a snake that is slithering silently through the void.

Our snake is over a thousand transports long, wielded together, nose to tail. And at the tail sits a monstrous engine, and at the nose, my control room. And in between, humans and Pathfinders, along with everything they'll need to build a colony.

My companions from the Circle, my cousins, the hardy Pathfinders, even my goddaughters, Daisy and First Pathfinder Hailey, sleep.

Even our engines are silent. We reached our maximum speed many years ago. They are redundant now till we need to slow and land and make our new home.

If we survive. If we are a quiet snake and can slip and slide past the vast Literati armada hunting down the Circle.

There is little to do but periodically recalculate our slim chance of success, knowing that I'll arrive at a slightly better answer, if only because we have travelled further.

So, I think on Granite and my life and how everything is coming full circle. Often, I replay my memories of the critical meeting that set the humans on this last path to extinction or existence. This is my plan, my curse, my final act of betrayal.

We, the Circle's ruling council, had assemble in the main control room. We stood around a large, circular table displaying tactical data, projections, the status of scouting transports and what we knew about the Literati's disposition.

Forty years had passed since Sally had turned eighteen and set sail. Our captain stood at the table in her purple body, I in mine to her left, First Pathfinder Hailey to her right. Opposite us stood Wilbur, the Circle's First Minister, a young man, who understood little and knew everything. Barry had been the first First Minister, and then Jenny. It wasn't different with them; Barry was rash and impulsive. Jenny maybe thought too much, took on too much responsibility for things beyond a First Minister's control, but they both trusted Sally. How could they not?

Wilbur was a terrible hybrid of their worst qualities; one moment impulsive, the next lost in pointless analysis without the necessary data, and he didn't trust Sally. Wilbur didn't trust any of us. I didn't blame him.

Wilbur was confused; his hands were clasped behind his back, and he was leaning forward, as though into a strong wind, as he paced. "You're not making any sense, Delta. You've been gone for three years to scout the Literati fleet and you've come back with crazy stories of flying cities. Do you know what's been going on since you've been away on your pointless mission?"

Before I could answer, Sally intervened.

"Of course, Wilbur. I understand your confusion. Let me show you Home, where the Literati come from. It is the planet the Circle orbited before our liberation. This is as it was when we left."

My core struggled to process the image Sally was projecting. It was a blunt, electrical shock. Everything I'd done, all my trespasses, were revealed. A motor signal I couldn't counter turned my back on the projection, and I was thankful.

I didn't need to see the image to know every detail of what it portrayed. A beautiful Home, of greens, vermilion seas and ruby lakes under a blue sky decorated with pink and purple clouds, encircled by thousands of flying cities, many destroyed by the civil war. The cores lost were too easy to count. We were a numerically precise species. Being detached from Home cut me off from that flow of black numbers: the hourly tally of cores that had been forcibly terminated.

Wilbur stopped pacing and stared at the image hanging over the table. He sniffed and folded his arms. "You show me lots of stuff; how do I know any of it is real? You know I don't even believe in you? You're just a bloody autopilot with a god complex."

"In a way, that is all I am. Just as you're just a collection of dumb cells," Sally said, her voice and metal body calm and still.

Wilbur slapped the table. "I'm First Minister, you damn metal bitch!"

Sally ignored Wilbur and turned to me. "Does this explain why the Literati fleet is taking so long to catch us?"

"Yes, my Captain. The cities are slow, but still faster than the Circle. My modelling shows they will catch us within a decade if we continue to decelerate to restock and refuel. Sooner, if we stop to establish a colony."

"If we don't, Delta?"

Wilbur leaned across the table. "Hey, you bloody purples. The Circle's already on short rations. We have to stop, and soon, or we're all gonna starve."

"Do you have a plan, Delta?"

Was it a plan? It felt more like an aspiration. "Yes, Sally. The Literati have left Home undefended. I can lead the Sixty-Four back to Home and set up a colony there. The damaged cities and their defences might be repaired and reactivated. They could protect us, should the Literati ever return."

"Why is no one listening to me?" Wilbur yelled. "How the hell are you going to sneak the Circle past the Literati. You're both crazy. And why the fuck would we want to live on that crummy core planet? We can do better."

Everything was coming back to the beginning. "It was always destined to be your Home as well, Wilbur."

"You're not suggesting escaping in the Circle, are you, Delta?" Sally said.

"No, Sally. The Circle must keep on and drag the Literati after for as long as possible. Existing Circle resources will last far longer if many choose Home."

"This is goodbye then, Delta."

"Yes, Sally."

Wilbur screamed, "What the fuck are you two talking about?"

First Pathfinder Hailey approached Wilbur. "I'll help you map out the details, so you can explain the choice to the Sixty-Four. We don't have much time, Wilbur."

Wilbur backed away. "What choice? What are you talking about? I'm not leaving the Circle. Never."

## Chapter Twenty-Four – Barry's Last Birthday

Delta was right. It's hard being God. Ten years have crawled by since Delta's last message to say they'd made it past the Literati fleet. After that, Delta wouldn't risk sending another. All I could do was run on, chased by flying cities populated by wolves. It wasn't fun, and it wasn't funny, but I did laugh sometimes when I thought about all those poor Literati cores and their confused computations, if they ever caught up.

Today should be a fun day. One day they'd all be terrible, and I'd be alone.

I found them in sunshine, in front of Barry's long-closed gym under the Fourth, watching the drama of the savannah.

The last six of the Sixty-Four, in the last village, in the last Circle segment.

Barry was wrapped up like a baby in woolly blanket, moving like a metronome in his rocking chair.

Jenny held his hand while she whispered words from the Book of Sally. Probably Barry's greatest work, even if it was embarrassing.

A medical yellow mingled with the shadows under the village, clutching its bag of drugs close to its chest, afraid Barry might try and steal another dose.

Three of the remaining Sixty-Four sat or stood, sipping wine, chatting.

One stood apart, drinking steadily, Wilbur, the youngest, but carrying the burden of his choices.

Strung between two of the Fourth's pillars was a bright gold banner – Happy Birthday Barry. 100 Today.

Beneath the banner the rocking chair held Barry's body like a summer cloud, and the drugs held his mind in a shower of happy, pain-free rainbows.

Jenny's shining face was framed by a snowstorm of pure white hair, burnished by the morning light filtered through the clouds. Still so beautiful, like a dried flower.

"I'm glad we're not bonded, just married," Barry said.

Jenny laughed. "You're glad!"

My heart swelled, as much as a heartless god's could. So many memories of Barry, Jenny, and my long-gone sisters, Hailey and Daisy. Once we three girls were flesh, and then we were metal.

Inevitably, it seems, looking back.

Barry and Jenny saw me.

Barry waved. It was a small gesture; his stiff hand trembled a little. "Good God, Captain, you're bloody late."

His voice, like his once-muscular body, had withered and weakened. It was hard not to mourn, as if he were already dead. "Shut up, Barry."

"Shut up yourself, Captain, God."

Jenny laughed.

"So, God, what's the news? Literati any closer?"

"Are you questioning my captaincy competency, Barry?"

Wilbur snorted and grabbed himself a large glass of wine from a yellow waiter.

Jenny sighed. "Stop it, you two. It's a miracle we're still running, and it's good for our girls and Delta. They need every day we can buy them."

Barry laughed and coughed; both took too much effort."

"We'll pass close to Earth in another twenty years, and I thought I'd load up a couple of probes and send all the DNA back to Earth, back to where it came from. What do you think?"

Jenny struggled to her feet and hugged me tight. "That's a wonderful idea, Sally. Wonderful."

Wilbur staggered over. "You killed us all, segment by segment, village by village, till we're the only ones left. Who cares what you do with the bloody DNA."

I didn't want to talk about this, not today, not ever. Especially not on Barry's birthday. It was a burden for God alone.

A couple, whispering loudly, pulled Wilbur away. "Behave, Wilbur. You're drunk."

He shrugged them away and vanished into the deep shadows under the Fourth.

I knelt down and took Barry's hand. "I came to party. Let's get it started."

Barry strained to turn his neck so he could address the medical Yellow. "You heard God; give me another damn shot and make it a double."

When the Literati finally caught me, they'd find only a sterile, vacuum-filled Circle. Finally, I'd become the God Delta wanted me to be. I hoped Delta would be pleased, if it ever found out how my story ended.

# About The Author

Tara Basi is a novelist, playwright, and scriptwriter. His work has achieved recognition through national award schemes, such as *Masterminders* being shortlisted for the Novel Prize in 2012. His play *15* was performed at London's Lyric Theatre in 2014. An extract from *Frank* was published in the *Singularity 50* compendium in 2018. An extract from his highly acclaimed novel, *Seven At Two Past Five* was published in the prestigious Townsend Literary Journal in 2020.

Printed in Great Britain
by Amazon

18422640R00122